DEATH IN DISGUISE

The black Marine Spetznas uniform was a decent enough fit. John Rourke closed the belt at his waist and slowed his pace, making his steps look more laborious to convince the Marine Spetznas Colonel that he and Darkwood had walked several miles to join up with him.

The Colonel said nothing for a moment, eyed them, and turned to Darkwood. "Your name, Corporal?"

"My name. Yes." Darkwood looked toward Rourke. "Can you imagine that? He wants my name."

John Rourke cleared his throat. "Excuse me, Corporal, may I give it to him?"

"Yes. Go ahead and give it to him," Darkwood said, stepping aside.

Rourke's right hand snaked toward the small of his back. He grabbed the Pachmayr-gripped butt of the .44 Magnum and knifed it forward, his finger already moving the trigger.

"Here it is, Colonel," Rourke said, and the 629 bucked in his fist.

THE SURVIVALIST SERIES
by Jerry Ahern

#1: TOTAL WAR   (2445, $2.95)

#2: THE NIGHTMARE BEGINS   (0810, $2.50)

#3: THE QUEST   (2670, $2.95)

#4: THE DOOMSAYER   (0893, $2.50)

#5: THE WEB   (2672, $2.95)

#6: THE SAVAGE HORDE   (1232, $2.50)

#7: THE PROPHET   (1339, $2.50)

#8: THE END IS COMING   (2590, $2.95)

#9: EARTH FIRE   (1405, $2.50)

#10: THE AWAKENING   (1478, $2.50)

#11: THE REPRISAL   (2393, $2.95)

#12: THE REBELLION   (1676, $2.50)

#13: PURSUIT   (1877, $2.50)

#14: THE TERROR   (1972, $2.50)

#15: OVERLORD   (2070, $2.50)

#18: THE STRUGGLE
JERRY AHERN

ZEBRA BOOKS
KENSINGTON PUBLISHING CORP.

This is a work of fiction. All the characters and events portrayed in this book are fictional, and any resemblance to real people or incidents is purely coincidental.

ZEBRA BOOKS

are published by

Kensington Publishing Corp.
475 Park Avenue South
New York, NY 10016

Copyright © 1989 by Jerry Ahern

First printing: February, 1989

Printed in the United States of America

For Larry Byars—
good friend and western memorabilia collector

Prologue

John Rourke stared through the Plexiglas panel which ran the length of the bottom portion of the portside fuselage door. There was nothing but snow and jagged jutting peaks and trenchlike rocky ravines, along the boundaries of these, and in patches bisecting the slopes some stands of pine trees. Above this, above the Soviet gunship which carried them away from the Second Chinese City's ruins, was a gray sky, laden with still more snow.

Riderless horses moved in bands of three or four, in some instances their Mongol riders—dead—dragged by a stirrup over the merciless terrain, the horses frightened off what trail there was, tacking at bizarre tangents over the ridgelines to escape the noise of the terrain-following helicopter.

There was a roar, the Plexiglas vibrating, the images of snow and boulders and all the rest—even the dead men dragged behind their animals—suddenly shimmering, a human scream rising from the explosion, then lost almost the same instant that it began, the Soviet gunship shuddering, a black-and-yellow fireball sweeping aft from the helicopter's cockpit chin bubble.

Vassily Prokopiev and Rourke's son Michael moved

as if they were a single entity, hurtling their bodies away from the aft belching flames. John Rourke was already moving, tearing one of the armored fire extinguishers from its mounting beside the fuselage door. He shouted, "Paul!" But the younger man was grabbing for the second extinguisher even as Rourke spoke.

Rourke swung toward Michael and Prokopiev, spraying their backs with the white stream of foam, Prokopiev rolling across the fuselage deck, the flames on Michael's trouser legs out, Michael whipping away one of the blankets covering the unconscious Chinese agent Han Lu Chen, smothering the flames racing over Prokopiev's tunic. Rourke shifted the extinguisher toward the cockpit, Paul Rubenstein already advancing against the flames. "No good, John!"

There was a humming sound, louder and louder, the gunship vibrating maddeningly around them as if it were going to shatter. Maria Leuden shrieked, "We are crashing!"

John Rourke thought, No shit, but said nothing, advancing against the flames. But Paul was right. No good. The extinguisher was dead in his hands and he threw it down. "Get Han!"

"My men!" Prokopiev shouted, starting forward, Michael bulldogging him. "I must—"

"They're dead, damn it, Vassily!" Michael insisted. As Rourke wheeled toward Han Lu Chen, he caught a glimpse of Michael shaking Prokopiev violently. In the next instant, the KGB Elite Corps Commander was up from his knees. "Help me!" Michael ordered Prokopiev.

Rourke's hands flew over the restraining buckles which bound Han Lu Chen into the webbing hammock, the Chinese beaten senseless by the torture masters of the Second City, comatose now. "Maria!

8

Get the weapons! Paul! You and Michael—get the fuselage door open and stand back—flames!" One of the safety strap buckles was stuck, Rourke's right hand grasping for the butt of the LS-X at his side, raking the primary edge over the strap, severing the fabric. As he sheathed the knife with his right hand, his left hand hauled Han Lu Chen up, Rourke putting his shoulder into him, then throwing the Chinese intelligence agent across his back.

There was a rush of frigid air, Michael shouting, "Look out!" A rush of fuel-scented heat filled the cabin.

As Rourke turned toward the fuselage door, tongues of flame were hungrily licking inward. "There's another extinguisher forward!" Paul Rubenstein shouted, streaking past Rourke, toward the inferno that was the cockpit.

"No!" John Rourke called after him, but his friend was gone, into the flames, then stumbling back, the third fire extinguisher tumbling from his fingers, rolling across the deck. Prokopiev was on him, flipping the extinguisher to Michael, then smothering the flames which assaulted Paul's legs and arms, beating them out. Maria Leuden dropped to her knees beside Prokopiev, using her coat to fight the flames.

Michael Rourke moved relentlessly forward, as-saulting the fire along the port side of the aircraft at its very heart, the overhead control panel, this the origin of the flames penetrating through the open fuselage door and blocking their egress.

There was a roaring wave of flame, and then the opening was clear. Michael yelled back, "Whatever we're doing, do it now!"

John Rourke stood beside the fuselage opening, the ground coming up fast, the gunship mere yards above the snow. There was no other choice. "Everybody!

9

Now! Follow me and jump! God help us!" Rourke looked back once, Paul Rubenstein scrabbling to his feet, Prokopiev and Maria Leuden helping him. There was no time to judge, to wait for a better spot. John Rourke shifted Han Lu Chen into his arms, shielding the unconscious man's head with his forearm, then jumped.

There was a rush of frigid air, Rourke's face and bare throat and hands pelted with spicules of ice and blowing snow, the incessant droning of the falling helicopter suddenly gone, Rourke's body impacting the snow-packed ground, his left hand covering Han's face, Rourke's body rolling, slamming hard to a stop, his breath knocked from him, his left wrist alive with pain as he moved it.

He looked up and back, brushing snow from his eyes with his right hand, Han moaning beneath him. Either Michael and Paul and the others had already jumped or . . . The Soviet gunship skipped over a rise of ground, rolled over and exploded, consumed in flame.

"Paul! Michael!"

Rourke was to his knees, still cradling Han Lu Chen in his arms. He stumbled forward, easing the Chinese into the snow, then got to his feet. When he moved his left wrist, it hurt, but nothing felt broken. Mechanically, he glanced at his Rolex. It was apparently unscathed. His whole left side, shoulder, rib cage, hip, and knee felt as if he'd been run over by something. He started forward, automatically reaching under his open parka for a gun. They had been shot down. "Michael! Paul! Maria! Prokopiev!"

"Dad!"

Rourke turned so quickly that his head began to swim and there were floaters in front of his eyes, his breathing still shallow, labored.

Michael was standing in the snow field a hundred

10

yards or so closer to the still burning gunship.

Rourke started toward his son . . .

Paul had sustained no serious new burns, nor had Prokopiev or Michael, although Maria Leuden's hands were slightly burned, but again not seriously. Han Lu Chen, oddly, seemed none the worse for the fall. As John Rourke and Michael Rourke advanced on four of the free-roaming Mongol horses, Rourke felt the stiffness leaving his left side, his left wrist still tender when he moved it wrong. But almost miraculously, no one had really been hurt, the only casualties the pilot and navigator who, Rourke judged, had likely died in the same instant as the explosion.

"That was a Soviet RPG that hit us, Michael."

"Some of the Second City Chinese," Michael Rourke said softly.

The horses were still better than a dozen yards away and to frighten them off now would simply mean more tracking and running and more time lost before they could reach the friendly German lines. A dying Mongol had evidently lashed himself into the saddle of his horse. Bony stumps and raw meat-appearing chunks of human body were tethered to one of the lathered animals at the end of a braided leather rope several feet behind one of the animals.

"Maybe Chinese, maybe Mongols," John Rourke said to his son after the protracted silence. "We'll be sitting ducks on horseback. We'll have to ride that long defile near the Soviet lines until we can separate from Prokopiev. If I were a Mongol, bent on revenge for the destruction of the Second City, I'd be waiting there. And that's what we were passing over when the RPG hit us. It's going to be you and me. Paul's too weak to do a lot of climbing and Prokopiev's not in such hot

11

shape either. Maria won't object if I borrow you a while, will she?"

"Do you like Maria?"

Rourke took his eyes from the horses for an instant—only that—and glanced toward his son. "She's pretty, she's smart, obviously nuts about you."

"You didn't answer my question."

"Do you love her?"

"Yeah."

"Then why don't you marry her? Because of what happened to your first wife and the baby?"

"Goddamnit, you don't mince words, do you, Dad?"

"I never had the time, or, the truth to tell, the inclination. So, I guess I don't 'mince words', Mike."

"That's about three times in my life you've called me that."

"You've got nothing better to do than keep count?" Rourke said rhetorically, smiling at Michael for a moment, then his eyes back on the horses.

"Yeah. Because of Madison and the baby," Michael almost whispered.

John Rourke said, "Get ready to go for the two nearest you. Remember—you're the one who told me these little horses are tough."

"You didn't answer my question."

"Do I like Maria? Sure. You treat her like shit. Now!" And John Rourke lunged toward the animals nearest him, his right fist closing on the bridle of the roan and his left hand grabbing the reins of the almost brindle-colored one. As the latter animal reared and Rourke sidestepped but held on, he felt as if his left wrist was breaking. But since it didn't, it provided further verification that it was only a minor sprain.

"Got mine," Michael shouted.

Rourke only nodded, despite the pain in his wrist, shifting the reins of both animals to his left hand. With his right hand he drew the Crain LS-X knife, cutting the dead man free . . .

The second time they caught Mongol horses, it was easier, but, that was partially because there were only two horses to catch. With them, they returned to where the other four horses and the other four members of their party were, unsaddling the animals, wiping them down, feeding them from the grain bags on each saddle. The saddles themselves, though quite ornate, reminded Rourke of the United States Army's McClellan saddles. They were split along the tree dead up the center. As with the Cavalry McClellans from the nineteenth century, the purpose for the split was obvious. In wintertime, the split would conduct heat from the animal's body to the body of the rider; in times of prolonged hard riding, when the animal would lose considerable body mass, the split would prevent gauling along the animal's spine. An old friend, a collector of western memorabilia, had explained the philosophy behind McClellan saddles to Rourke five centuries ago.

Taking the sturdiest of the horses for themselves, leaving Maria and Paul and Prokopiev to ride down through the defile with the injured Han Lu Chen, John and Michael Rourke started for the higher ground. Soviet assault rifles were lashed to the saddles of their expropriated animals, Mongol swords lashed to the saddles as well. One of the dead Mongols, whose body was still in the saddle when his animal was captured, had carried a five-centuries-old Glock-17 and several spare magazines. Rourke found the gun totally serviceable after administering a thorough cleaning while the horses rested, then left it with Prokopiev, replacing the corroded ammunition with some of the

13

modern German ammunition manufactured for him to duplicate the 115-grain Federal 9mm BP.

Once they reached German lines, proper emergency care could be found, Rourke having done all that he could for Han Lu Chen without any real facilities at his disposal. And transport could be gotten to the First Chinese City and its modern hospital.

As they rode, they talked, about Annie, for whom they both were worried, about Natalia's problems. As they crossed into a snow-drifted ravine, they were forced to dismount and lead the animals. "If these animals were larger, this would be easier," Michael Rourke exhaled, tugging at the Mongol animal as it began to founder in a suddenly deeper drift. The snow still fell. And suddenly Michael Rourke asked his father, "You talk about me and Maria—what about you and Natalia?"

"What do you mean exactly?" Rourke responded, walking alongside his horse, holding the reins, pushing against the animal's flanks to propel it ahead.

"You're in love with two women; two women are in love with you. What are you going to do about it?"

John Rourke looked at his son, smiling, saying, "You have any solutions in mind?"

"No," Michael said almost desultorily.

"Well, neither do I. I know Natalia's mental collapse is at least partially my fault, maybe all my fault—"

"I didn't say that, Dad," Michael interrupted.

"Stating the obvious is a waste of time; and I've never accused you of being a time-waster, Michael. I know something has to be done, but if I already knew what, I would have done it. Centuries ago."

They reached the height of the defile and the snow was less deep here and they were able to remount the Mongol horses. Rourke looked at his Rolex, computing the amount of time it would take for Paul and the others to reach the danger zone. And he spurred his mount ahead . . .

Ahead of them lay a ridgeline that resembled the backbone of some monstrously large prehistoric beast, and between the rocky vertebrae were huddled at best count from the distance at which Rourke observed perhaps a dozen and a half men. All of them that he could see through the German binoculars were Mongols, armed variously with twentieth century automatic rifles and a few captured Soviet arms, among these at least one more RPG of the type used to shoot down the Soviet gunship aboard which Rourke and his son and all the rest had nearly died. The position which the Mongols held on the ridgeline dominated the gorge which had to be crossed through to reach the Russian or German lines.

John Rourke lay prone in the snow on a flat promontory of rock overlooking the ridge and the gorge below. In a normal springtime, if there were such things still, the gorge would likely be a torrent. But, as it was, a stream approximately a dozen yards wide at most cut violently down the center of the gorge, whitewater splashing out of wide, deep-looking pools, in the smaller pools surface ice formed, starkly white beneath the gray sky.

On either side of the gorge a man could lead a horse, but only a desperate fool or a person with a death wish would have ridden one there, the surface too uneven.

Michael, lying beside him, spoke. "How soon?"

"Tell you in a second," Rourke almost whispered, shifting position, scanning along the length of the gorge with his binoculars, at last finding the party of horsemen, the German binoculars automatically adjusting focus as Rourke depressed the focus button. In

15

another quarter mile, Paul and the others would be forced to dismount, be such easy prey that even the most lackluster marksman armed with an assault rifle of even marginal quality could pin them down and eventually kill them.

He refocused on the Mongols along the ridgeline. For a moment, his mind was drawn back to his early boyhood, when the radio would be turned on and he would hear the thunder of hoofbeats, the crack of pistol shots. The Lone Ranger. He had followed the program almost religiously on radio and then on television. What he saw below him reminded him of the massacre of the Texas Rangers in the origin story of the Masked Man, evil killers lying in wait for slaughter. But John Rourke and his son Michael were in position to stop a bloodbath of innocents, to ambush the ambushers.

"We have to hurry, Michael. They'll be into that gorge on foot before we know it." And John Rourke cased the binoculars, then on knees and elbows worked his way back from the edge . . .

In the spate of superspy films in the middle and late 1960s, there was always a suppressor or silencer handy when the situation required silence. Given the time and some basic, otherwise innocuous materials, John Rourke could have built such a device. But there was no time and such once ordinary items as orange juice cans or power mower mufflers or even potatoes (at least in this icy wilderness) no longer existed.

What needed doing was a job for a knife.

Stripped of all firearms except for his twin Detonics mini guns, the two Scoremasters and the Smith & Wesson revolver at his right hip, John Rourke moved as quietly as he could up the back of the ridge. There was evidence of considerable erosion here and he moved through a chest-deep rill, at times forced to place one foot directly in front of the other because the rill was so sharply V-ed.

He could not see Michael, Michael moving up from the opposite side of the ridgeline, likely not as high yet because there had been greater distance for Michael to travel to his starting point. But the ridge was lower farther west, so with any luck Michael should reach the top at approximately the same time John Rourke did. Rourke had set a precise time for the process of removing the Mongols from the ridgeline to begin, whether both he and his son were in place or not. Much after that, and it might be too late.

Clenched tight in John Rourke's right fist was the Crain Life Support System X . . .

Less than ten feet from him, the nearest of the Mongols lay in wait. From just below the ridge where Rourke hid, he could see that his initial estimate of their numbers seemed close to correct—about eighteen of them. Even in the bitter cold of the thin mountain air, when the wind blew in the right direction, the man's smell was like that of an animal fresh from rolling in its own excrement. In the man's hands was a Soviet assault rifle, beside him a half dozen spare magazines for the weapon and a single Soviet high explosive grenade.

Rourke glanced at the black face of the Rolex Submariner on his left wrist.

It would be time in less than a minute.

Rourke reached to the small of his back, unsheathing the A.G. Russell Sting IA Black Chrome, the Crain knife still in his right hand.

His eyes traveled to the second hand of the Rolex.

Time.

Rourke rose to his full height, coming up over the lip of the ridgeline in a dead run, cutting the distance to the Mongol by half before the man began to turn around. As the Mongol opened his mouth to shout a warning or a scream, the tip of the LS-X entered him—in the mouth, punching through the back of the neck as Rourke thrust, severing the Mongol's spinal column.

Rourke wrenched the blade free, the body falling, gravel crunching, the Mongol nearest looking around, raising the pistols in his hands, wheeling toward Rourke as Rourke lunged, the Crain knife impaling the man just below the right breast, Rourke drawing the man up and toward him on the knife, raking the smaller Sting IA across the right side of the Mongol's throat, Rourke turning away as the blood sprayed, with his right foot kicking the Mongol off the blade of the Crain knife.

Rourke let the smaller knife fall from his left hand, shifting the LS-X from his right, then drawing the .44 Magnum revolver from the Milt Sparks flap holster at his right hip. As another of the Mongols spun toward him, Rourke double-actioned the 629, the six-inch tubed Smith rocking in his fist, the Mongol taking the hit, going down, rolling. Rourke was on him as the Mongol drew his pistol to fire, the upper left side of his torso drenched in blood, the Mongol dying but too stubborn to let go. Rourke backhanded the Crain knife's primary edge from the left cheekbone and down across the Adam's apple, severing the windpipe.

A burst of assault rifle fire hammered into the rocks near him, Rourke hurtling the LS-X down like a spike into the dying Mongol's chest, punching the 629 forward, firing once, then again and again, the Mongol firing at him from fifty feet away falling, sprawling back.

Rourke could see Michael, Michael's knife hacking wildly outward, half severing the arm of one of the Mongols, Michael stepping into him, the Beretta in Michael's left fist firing again and again, punching the body away as Michael turned toward the next man.

Rourke emptied the 629 as his left hand ripped one of the twin stainless Detonics mini-guns from the double Alessi shoulder rig, his thumb jacking the hammer back, his right hand holstering the 629 as the first round from the Detonics .45 was fired. As he fired the second round, one of the Mongols grasping his abdomen and going down, Rourke's right hand swept cross body, his fist closing on the Pachmayr-gripped butt of the second Detonics, the first emptying as he cleared the second gun from the leather, jerked the hammer back and fired.

The slide still locked back empty, he thrust the Detonics mini-gun into the waistband of his trousers, his left hand moving inches, tugging free one of the Scoremasters, firing out the Detonics Combat Master in his right hand, dropping it into the hip pocket of his pants, drawing the second Scoremaster as he fired the first.

The heavy claps of his .45s, the lighter, sharper cracks of Michael's Beretta 92Fs.

And no more of the Mongols remained alive to kill.

Chapter One

The day-lights which glowed from within the high dome of the flower-shaped First City's administrative Petal normally appeared to the naked eye as natural as sunlight. Now, the lights flickered maddeningly, reminding John Rourke fleetingly of the cheap urban neon signs which only he and few others still alive could remember. No great loss. These lights cast sinister shadows over the pain-etched faces of the wounded who lay everywhere, like broken and discarded dolls flung aside by some careless child in a fit of temper.

All about them as they walked, Rourke saw death, suffering and incalculable physical damage, from the most heroically posed shattered statue to a trampled garden of once exquisitely delicate flowers, from blackened, explosion-cratered streets and walkways where normal lives and commerce had been conducted instants before the carnage to the glitter and crunch beneath their booted feet of the shattered glass from now windowless buildings. Chinese troops in irregular numbers, attired in ragged, smoke-smudged uniforms, ran to reinforce defensive positions against renewed attack while others aided the men and women in dirty and bloodstained hospital attire who tended the civilians and military personnel who had some even slight chance to be saved.

Rourke's son Michael, and Maria Leuden, the German archaeologist who was Michael's mistress, had left Rourke and Rubenstein as they had entered the city, personally placed the Chinese Intelligence Agent Han Lu Chen on a commandeered monorail car so he could be speeded to the medical center. Han's injuries were grave, sustained at the hands of the barbarians in the Second City, requiring the sort of immediate medical attention that under the circumstances could only be gotten if forced.

John Thomas Rourke dropped to one knee beside an old woman who lay beside an overturned flower cart, her inner thigh bleeding heavily. But the bleeding was not arterial. He applied pressure with his fingertips and the flow of blood eased as a Chinese soldier who evidently spoke no English but recognized him nodded, said, "Rourke," and smiled, then continued plowing through a medical kit of the type used in the field by the Defense Forces of the First City. The private soldier at last found what he sought and began to apply a pressure bandage, Rourke nodding to Paul Rubenstein who bent over beside them, dropped to his knees, helped the soldier with the proper application of the dressing. Paul had seen him—Rourke—do it often enough, Rourke supposed. And Paul Rubenstein had hands that were good, obeyed him well, were strong, and a mind quick to learn.

The bandage in place, the old woman's eyelids flickered, shy dark eyes probing his and Rubenstein's face; and her frail hands clutched at theirs, inadvertently smearing her hands with her own blood. Rourke smiled down at her, stood to his feet, wiped his hands clean of the blood, then picked up his parka and began walking again, Paul beside him. Paul's right arm was crudely slung with a shirt-sleeve, much of the not-too-badly burned area exposed, but none of the Chinese stopping to marvel at the wound, because so many of the Chinese were themselves wounded.

There had been heavy fighting here in the First Chinese City. P.A. systems blared instructions in Chinese, the words Rourke understood for "wounded" and "dead" repeated often.

Rourke kept walking.

At last, he and Paul Rubenstein reached the steps of the government building. An immaculately dressed woman in modestly high heels and equally modestly slitted chong-san waited at the base of the steps, the look of distraction bordering on frenzy in the eyes set in her otherwise serene face unnerving. Rourke recognized her, a personal aid to the Chinese Chairman. The epicanthic lids closed and opened, the movement like the fluttering of a bird's wing. She was very beautiful.

The Chinese/English interpreter told him in her singsong soprano voice, an unreal but somehow sincere smile on her carefully made-up face, "The helicopter which purportedly carried your daughter, Doctor Rourke, and Major Tiemerovna and Captain Hammerschmidt—it has unfortunately not been heard from and is presumed to be lost somewhere over the Yellow Sea."

John Thomas Rourke began running as she uttered the word "unfortunately," tossed aside his parka and other temporarily unnecessary gear as she said the simple word "lost." As he reached the steps leading into the government building, taking them three at a time in a dead run, Paul Rubenstein was beside him. Rourke glanced at his friend as the woman's voice behind them droned on. "A Soviet helicopter reportedly was encountered and there was an exchange of fire and—"

"I know" was all Rourke said, not in response to the spoken condolences of the female interpreter but to the unspoken words of Paul Rubenstein beside him. Annie, Rourke's daughter, was Paul's wife.

Rourke reached the height of the steps, running faster now, Paul nearly staying abreast of him. Rourke merely eyed the First City guards who momentarily interposed themselves in the open doorway, not needing to shove past them because they moved aside before him unbidden.

Rourke saw his wife Sarah standing at the head of the staircase, legs spread apart, face smudged. The staircase widened gradually, leading upward from the far end of the great hall through which Rourke and Rubenstein ran, upward toward the executive offices. A pistol was belted to Sarah's pregnancy-swollen midsection, a black T-shirt visible beneath an open German camouflage BDU blouse.

"There's been no word, John. No word at all."

"Are you sure they went down over water, weren't blown up when the missiles or whatever struck?"

He was taking the staircase like a hill, charging up its midsection, taking Sarah into his arms as he reached the top.

"I'm afraid, John."

John Rourke held his wife in his arms, tightly.

Forcing himself to walk rather than run because she was beside him was the most difficult thing he had ever done. And Paul Rubenstein walked with them . . .

"But Comrade Colonel—"

"Ground forces." With more ground forces he could have conquered. Nicolai Antonovitch walked quickly over the freeze-hardened, snow-packed ground, extemporizing orders to the aide who almost ran beside him. "Withdraw all functional personnel and equipment from the area surrounding the Second Chinese City, leaving only what is necessary to cover withdrawal of the wounded. Whatever the nature of the explosion there, it has likely neutralized the preponderance of their forces. I want to be able to attack the First City in full strength within twelve hours from now. They must still reel from the blow they have already sustained. Order the commander of our army in Lydveldid Island to consolidate his forces within the Hekla volcanic cone itself and to abandon, then destroy the German Base outside Hekla. I want a full airborne assault force ready to move at a moment's notice against Eden Base in American Georgia. I want that force ready within twelve hours. A coordinated attack will further sap German military strength. I fly to the Underground City. For troops."

Antonovitch quickened his pace to a run, his gunship's rotor blades turning, snow swirling cyclonically in their downdraft. There was one other possibility, if he could carry it off without losing everything. If he could make contact . . .

Louise Walenski was smiling like an idiot, almost laughing as she bumped into him. "Excuse me! Sir."

Jason Darkwood was halfway over the flange for the watertight door leading to the *Reagan*'s bridge when he noticed her eyes. "Is something wrong, Lieutenant? Do I have my shoes on backward or something?" She laughed, running the free hand that didn't hold her clipboard back through her pretty hair. He wasn't wearing shoes at all, of course, but rather issue combat boots as he always wore with his Class B uniform. "Lieutenant?"

"Ohh, nothing, sir—I ahh—I was just really pleased that we caught onto that transponder signal in time to get them all out of the water. I think Lieutenant Mott did a great job with tracking. And Lieutenant Bowman, too, of course. Where would Communications have been without Navigation, after all."

"Words to ponder indeed, Lieutenant." Darkwood continued on his way, through the companionway, through the next watertight doorway, and to the Con.

Lieutenant Junior Grade Arturo Rodriguez sang out, "Captain's on the bridge!"

The *Reagan*'s bridge crew started to attention, or what was left of them, anyway; Darkwood called out the anticipated "Carry on," then proceeded toward his command chair as the bridge personnel looked back to their stations.

Not only was his warfare officer, Lieutenant Walenski, missing, but so were Lieutenants Junior Grade Kelly and Bowman. Darkwood sat down, ran his fingers over the console arms, and looked at Sebastian, his tall, leanly muscled First Officer leaning over the illuminated plotting board. "Mr. Sebastian?"

"Aye, sir?" Sebastian answered.

"Where are the female members of the bridge crew? I literally bumped into Lieutenant Walenski—back there," and he gestured behind him.

"You pose an interesting question, Captain" was all Sebastian responded.

"Interesting question," Darkwood nodded. "Do you have an interesting answer?"

"No, sir. Not at all. The answer isn't that terribly interesting at all."

Darkwood stood up, took the three steps down, and stood leaning against the First Officer's chair. "Even if it isn't interesting, Mr. Sebastian, share it with me anyway."

Lieutenant Commander T.J. Sebastian's eyes shifted quickly aft along the bridge and then to Darkwood's face, Sebastian's brown hands distending over the illuminated surface of the chart table as if it were one of the tactile sensitive video games with which television news broadcasters contended teenagers at Mid-Wake were obsessed. "Actually, Jason, surprise!"

Darkwood started to speak when he heard laughter behind him, then Margaret Barrow's voice. "Congratulations, Jason—Captain Jason Darkwood, Captain U.S.S. *Ronald Wilson Reagan*." She held a radio-fax transcription in her left hand. Radio-fax messages were only possible when the ship was surfaced.

Behind him, he heard the click of the microphone which Sebastian used when relaying orders from the bridge. "Attention all hands; now hear this. This is First Officer Sebastian speaking." Captain? Darkwood thought. He was Captain of the *Reagan* well enough, but his rank was— He started to interrupt Sebastian. But Sebastian kept on talking, his voice echoing back through the open watertight doors, piped over the entire ship, Darkwood realized. "I have the honor to announce the promotion of Commander Jason Darkwood to the rank of Captain, with all honors and privileges pertaining thereto. All personnel performing nonessential ship's functions, ten-hut!"

Margaret Barrow handed him the radio-fax, Department of the Navy orders signed by Admiral Rahn and countersigned by President Fellows, which wasn't necessary to make the orders of promotion official but was quite an honor. More of an honor, though, was the collection of signatures on the reverse of the radio-fax. Every officer and man of the *Reagan*.

Sebastian held the microphone in his left hand, rose to his full height—which was substantial—and saluted. "Captain Darkwood. The microphone, sir." He offered the microphone.

Darkwood took it, stared at it a moment.

"Go ahead, Jason," Sebastian smiled.

Darkwood still didn't know what to say. "This is—the Captain speaking, I suppose. Well. I really am a Captain. Not just a Captain. Nuts. A man couldn't ask for a better crew. I've just been handed the radio-fax all of you signed. I know I'll receive the official document once we return to Mid-Wake, but this is the copy that I'll always treasure. Lest I have to remind anyone, we have a submarine to run and our Soviet friends would be more than happy to take it off our hands if we let them. Thank you. Thank you all very much. Return to your stations."

Darkwood handed the microphone back to Sebastian. Sebastian said, "The Captain is receiving his cake." Darkwood looked at Sebastian, then looked toward Margaret Barrow. Behind the ship's doctor stood his Warfare, Sonar, and Navigation officers, Warfare holding an impossibly large sheet cake with chocolate frosting on top and Sonar and Navigation holding plates, napkins, and a funny-looking knife Darkwood assumed was designed for cutting cakes. "Slices will be available during the regular mess schedule. That is all."

"It's hot, sir," his Warfare officer warned him.

"I'll take that into consideration, Lieutenant," Darkwood nodded, smiling, feeling embarrassed and slightly tongue-tied. Sam Aldridge and Tom Stanhope appeared on the bridge behind his female bridge personnel, Aldridge grinning, laughing both at him and with him.

Margaret Barrow leaned up and kissed him on the cheek. "I've got that Russian woman to look after, Jason. All the best." And she turned and ran off, past Walenski and the cake that had been decorated too hurriedly; frosting was gooing in the middle where the temperature was still too warm and all the bridge crew knotted around her.

"Ahh—"

"Captain. May I suggest that Lieutenant Walenski continue her supervision of the cake and undertake its equitable distribution to all members of the bridge crew and the remainder of the ship's company after you have made the initial cut?"

Jason Darkwood wasn't quite certain what Sebastian had said, but he agreed with it anyway and Lieutenant Junior Grade Bowman smiled at him as she handed him the odd-looking knife . . .

A piece of cake on a saucer in his left hand, Jason Darkwood pushed through the door into Margaret Barrow's sick bay, past Lieutenant Stanhope's Marine guard, telling the corporal, "As you were." The young girl (a Rourke) who'd been the only one conscious when the *Reagan* had surfaced answering the transponder now lay asleep—sedated, he guessed—on one of the beds, at the opposite end of sick bay from the Russian woman. Darkwood had never seen the Rourke girl before, but he had seen the Russian woman. The Rourke girl—her name was Annie Rubenstein—was exceedingly beautiful. The Russian woman, Major Tiemerovna, was exquisite. Tossing and turning as she was beneath the blanket, restraints crisscrossing the bed, she looked somehow very tragic. In the third occupied bed was a man, resting comfortably it appeared. Obviously military, he looked like a blond and blue-eyed version of black-skinned, brown-eyed Sam Aldridge.

Margaret Barrow came out of her office.

"Brought me my cake?"

"Brought you your cake," Darkwood nodded. "It's very good. Taking the welfare of the crew as my utmost concern, as I always do, I realized it'd be necessary to have two pieces myself just to make certain it was entirely suitable. Then I carefully checked with Sam Aldridge, who, as it turned out, is quite the connoisseur of cake. He liked it, too."

"Well, if the Marine Corps approves, gee-whiz."

"How are your patients?"

She tasted the cake. "Mmm—it is good. Well, let's see. Machinist First Class Hong—he had the blood blister, remember? Well—"

Darkwood smiled. "Right. Hong's a fine man. I was more concerned about women."

"You never change," she smiled too sweetly. "Let's see. Mrs. Rubenstein voluntarily accepted a sedative once I told her that Major Tiemerovna was stable and that she'd be of greater value to the Major if she were well rested once the Major awakened."

"How about Major Tiemerovna?"

"That's another story altogether, Jason. I'm no psychiatrist, but from what Mrs. Rubenstein told me, Major Tiemerovna's a pretty sick woman."

"Give me a best guess."

She shrugged her shoulders and eyebrows in unison. It looked kind of sexy, Darkwood thought absently. But Margaret Barrow always looked kind of sexy anyway. "It probably started as what you or I would call a psychosis—"

"I use that word all the time. Tell me in easy to understand words, Maggie."

She shrugged—just her shoulders this time—as she perched on the edge of a surgery table. "From what Mrs. Rubenstein said and from my own limited observations, the Major seems to be suffering, among other things, from manic depression, but locked into the depressive state. Like I said, I'm no shrink. She's a very sick woman. Total disorientation, obviously experiencing hallucinations, catatonic most of the time. There's nothing I can do for her except monitor vital functions, keep her cleaned and bathed and sedated until we reach port. In layman's language, she's gone off the deep end, Jason. And after what she's evidently been through—some sort of battle, as Mrs. Rubenstein put it."

"'. . . some sort of battle,'" Darkwood repeated.

"And the man?"

"He's Captain of Commandos Otto Hammerschmidt of the Republic of New Germany in Argentina. That's what he said before I sedated him. And he's got very fast hands," she smiled. "He's going to be all right, though."

"One of the reconstructed Nazis, huh."

"That's not nice to say, Jason!"

"Fine."

His ship's company now included a German officer, the daughter of the twice legendary hero Doctor John Thomas Rourke, and a Major in the Soviet KGB who was gorgeous even if she was looney at the moment, both women five centuries old and 'holding.'

And the *Reagan* was farther away from Mid-Wake than he wanted to consider.

He asked Margaret Barrow, "You wouldn't like to come to my cabin and celebrate my promotion, would you?"

She leaned back and rocked on one heel. "How?"

"I meant maybe just a cup of coffee and some conversation."

"You want to be treated for mental illness, too?"

He smiled. "Can't blame a guy for trying, Maggie."

She smiled back. "I'd blame me if you succeeded. But yeah, I'll come. If it's more than coffee."

"Are you suggesting we examine and possibly test the medicinal liquor stores to confirm that no chemical breakdown has taken place which might alter its effectiveness?"

"Who'd you get that line from?"

"I've been studying circumlocution with Sebastian." And she laughed and came into his arms. Darkwood's eyes drifted toward Major Natalia Anastasia Tiemerovna. He'd learned firsthand that she was one hell of a woman.

He looked away.

A transponder signal relayed to him, the transponder given to Doctor Rourke when he left Mid-Wake, as an emergency device, the signal picked up on satellite buoys. A terse message from Mid-Wake command to respond. A search that was less than an hour, but seemed like more to pinpoint the source of the transponder. One of those helicopters on the bottom, shot all to hell it appeared. On the surface of the Yellow Sea, two women and a man, only one of them conscious (the young woman) and keeping the others afloat.

She had her father's guts, certainly.

And clinging to them just as dearly as the human beings were the weapons. More antiques, not dissimilar to what Doctor Rourke carried, his Detonics .45s.

Why was the helicopter shot down? Had the war on the surface of the Earth which Doctor Rourke had told them about and which they had experienced first hand for a brief time heated up?

The Rourke girl—Mrs. Rubenstein—had seemed past exhaustion, but hadn't seemed anywhere near to giving up.

Surface dwellers were strange, certainly, but in many ways they were little different from the people of Mid-Wake. They were driven to survival, and driven *by* it.

"What are you thinking, Jason?" Margaret Barrow asked, pushing a little way from him. "It isn't about me, is it?"

"No. But it isn't about anyone else." He looked at her and smiled. "Are you going to eat the rest of that cake? I mean, it would be a sin to let it go to waste after all the effort everyone put into making it."

She turned around, took the plate off her desk, and handed it to him, but she didn't say, "If that doesn't take the cake." He would have.

Chapter Two

Colonel Wolfgang Mann, de facto supreme commander of German forces in the field, stood, the tips of his splayed fingers touching to the tabletop, its black mirror finish reflecting a distorted image of him as he spoke. "The Soviet offensive is continuing. I have just received a communiqué that Soviet forces have consolidated their position in Lydveldid Island, within the Hekla Community itself, and have totally destroyed our base outside Hekla. Soviet troops are apparently massing for another attack on Eden Base. Meanwhile, a small but very mobile force continues to harass efforts in New Germany to resupply forces in the field and, because of the presence of this force, substantial reinforcement of our troops in the field is out of the question. Yet, we have sustained significant casualties. In the same report from our installation outside Eden Base, to which I alluded a moment ago, I was informed that the Japanese Lieutenant Kurinami was reported shot down in battle against the Soviets during a raid on their staging area. Kurinami is missing and presumed dead. As concerns the whereabouts of Frau Rubenstein, Fraulein Major Tiemerovna, and Captain Hammerschmidt, I have fifteen helicopters and three J7-Vs in the air over the Yellow Sea searching for the downed gunship or even some sign of wreckage. So far, there is no sign."

The Chairman of the First Chinese City rose from his black lacquer chair, several dark bruises visible on his face, his normally patent-leather-looking hair slightly disarranged, his eyes weary. "So many things, Doctor Rourke, have been done by you and your family for our people. I am ashamed I can do no more than offer you what meager resources still remain at my disposal."

He had said nothing, everything. John Rourke tented his fingers to keep his hands from trembling. Michael Rourke, Maria Leuden beside him, entered the conference room unannounced. He looked at his son and the German archaeologist. Michael took a seat at the far end of the table, Maria standing beside his chair. Her devotion to Michael bordered on slavishness, but Rourke pushed the thought of that away. His son's relationship with the woman—pleasant, intelligent—was none of his business.

Paul Rubenstein, his injuries properly attended to, his face grim, softly thudded his left fist against the table as Sarah Rourke spoke. "I think I can speak for my daughter Ann even though her husband is present." And she looked at Paul Rubenstein, touched her hand to his. "I think Annie and Natalia and Captain Hammerschmidt are alive out there, even considering what my husband told you about Natalia's present state of mental collapse. I realize that the war effort is for the greater good and I realize you can't keep combing the same stretch of ocean for them. They wouldn't want you to. I guess that's what I'm trying to say. I don't want to say it. But I think they'd want me to say it anyway." She looked down into her lap, or perhaps toward the baby she carried inside her.

"I may have a potential solution to all of our problems," John Rourke said so softly he almost spoke in a whisper. "I gave Annie something when she boarded the helicopter. It was a special transponder given to me by the naval authorities of Mid-Wake. It's the same device issued to their Marine commandos and naval frogmen as part of their survival kits. It has a destruct device built into it which can be activated in the event of capture, of course. But, when used as intended, it's designed to broadcast a special low-frequency homing beacon that can be picked up by communications buoys the people of Mid-Wake use in much the same manner persons of my era utilized communications satellites. That frequency is computer monitored twenty-four hours per day. If Annie had the time to activate the frequency, there's a substantial possibility that the reason no sign of survivors from the crash of the gunship has been found on the surface is that there are no survivors on the surface."

The Chairman said, "Do you imply, Doctor—"

"Yes. They may be aboard a U.S. submarine operating out of Mid-Wake," Rourke answered, cutting him off. "I have no means of contacting Mid-Wake, at least not directly. But if I can have a German gunship, Colonel Mann," and Rourke looked across the table toward the German commander, "and enough fuel, I can reach the approximate area of open water beneath which Mid-Wake is located. If you can loan me a very powerful conventional explosive—" And Rourke used the word "conventional" intentionally, because he knew the Germans were working on a nuclear device in the event the Russians gained access to such weapons and used them. "A powerful conventional explosive detonated on the surface above Mid-Wake would be bound to be picked up on their sensors. They'll come to investigate and I'll make

35

contact. If they have picked up Annie and Natalia and Captain Hammerschmidt, I'll know at once. And, if they haven't, then perhaps with their help— I don't know. We'll keep looking. No matter how long we have to. And their submarines can help. Anyway— But either way," and Rourke exhaled, studied his hands for a moment, "I may be able to effect some sort of alliance with the government of Mid-Wake. With the aid of their underwater technology we could introduce a wild card—"

"A 'wild card,' Herr Doctor?" Mann queried.

"Something unsuspected in its true nature, beyond what would be expected ordinarily, Colonel. We could introduce such a wild card into the war against the Soviets and if we used it effectively, knock them out. It's only a matter of time before Colonel Antonovitch or the Soviet leadership of the Underground City—and perhaps by now with Karamatsov's death they're working together—but it's only a matter of time until someone from the Soviet faction on the surface successfully makes a second contact with the Soviet underwater complex and works out an alliance. These Soviet forces have considerable nuclear capabilities, as we've discussed before. If Antonovitch were able to introduce such capabilities as a wild card of his own, we'd lose."

"I can provide such a helicopter, Herr Doctor," Mann volunteered.

"It'll need amphibious capabilities, and as much as I'd like to strip it of weapons so we'd be able to fly faster and farther between refuelings, we'll be over Soviet waters much of the time and there's no telling what we'll encounter. So, conversely, I'll need all the weapons we can pack aboard." He looked at Paul Rubenstein. "Come with?"

"You couldn't stop me, John; not even you," the

younger man smiled.

"Dad—"

Rourke looked toward his son. "No. You'll be needed to help Colonel Mann. And to take care of your mother." Sarah started to speak and he knew what she'd say. Rourke told her, "If I were Colonel Mann, I'd keep a minimal presence in Iceland outside Hekla just to keep the Russians bottled up, then hit their staging area near Eden Base in Georgia. If the Russians can be forced out, the German installation outside Eden Base can become a staging area along the German supply route."

"My plan exactly, Herr Doktor," Mann nodded, lighting a cigarette from his case.

"And you and the baby will be safer with Colonel Mann's forces, either here or in New Germany. I'm not about to lose everyone I care for, and even though there's a substantial possibility for success of the mission, in the event of failure, failure will be fatal."

"No, damn it, John!"

Rourke lit the cigar he'd set on the table beside his tented fingers. "Yes. You're not coming with Paul and me. It's too dangerous. No purpose would be served by endangering you more than you have been already. It's dangerous enough just staying here or going to New Germany. I know you want to come and I know why. For the same reason I'm going. But you're not." And John Rourke stood up.

"John!"

He didn't look at his wife, simply told her, "No."

Chapter Three

At times, the oppressive gray clouds, already partially obscured by the heavy white flakes of snow which seemed to fall unendingly from them onto the Earth below, were almost totally blocked by squadrons of black-skinned Soviet gunships.

The drifts lay deeper in the ravine which he followed, and Akiro Kurinami's movements were slowed because of them; but, on the higher ground, there was the very real danger of being spotted from the air by the still-massing Russian helicopters.

And time was of the essence. The growing Soviet armada would soon attack Eden Base.

The distance to Eden Base was more miles than Kurinami wanted to contemplate, but John Rourke's Retreat was vastly closer.

At Rourke's Retreat, there was a powerful radio with which he could contact the German installation outside Eden Base, pass along intelligence on Soviet strength. If the Soviets attacked without the forces of New Germany knowing the heightened numbers in their fleet, the Russians would surely achieve total military victory in what, Before the Night of the War, had been The United States, and Eden Base would be overrun. The space shuttles themselves would be destroyed, their computer records seized or, worse still, erased. The frozen embryonic life forms of animals and birds, the botanical cuttings and seeds—much of the future of life on Earth would vanish from the Earth forever. The Chinese, as Kurinami understood it, and the Germans, of course, had used their underground shelters as environmental arks as well as circumstances allowed, as had the Icelandics (spared by a freak effect of the Van Allen Radiation Belts) utilized their network of geo-thermal-powered pockets of civilization within the Arctic wasteland that now blanketed the Earth to well below sixty degrees North Latitude. But nowhere on Earth now, since the destruction of all surface life, did many of the species exist which existed in Eden Project stores, which could be returned to Earth. And the knowledge in the Eden computers was the accumulated knowledge of the centuries and irreplaceable.

Eden Base had to be saved at all costs.

And John Rourke's Retreat was the only hope.

Freezing cold, hungry, exhausted, Akiro Kurinami raised his feet another time, then another and another and another. In his mind's eye, he put the face of Elaine Halversen ahead of him, going on ever toward her . . .

It was becoming increasingly difficult to leave New Germany, Dodd knew, and these disciples of the dead leader might well be the last he could count on for help until the Soviet offensive was crushed.

In the uncompleted permanent structures construction zone, a chemical heater providing warmth enough that hoods of parkas could be lowered, Christopher Dodd stood as part of a ragged semicircle around the heat source. Damien Rausch, the apparent leader of the Germans, lit a cigarette. Rausch was tall, broad-shouldered, and the muscled neck bespoke strength and fitness. His voice, as he spoke, was a sonorous baritone, the English devoid of any accent as far as Christopher Dodd could detect. "You seem to misunderstand the circumstances, Herr Commander. We were not sent here to this inhospitable wasteland to obey your orders. I have my orders, and with the help of my men shall carry them out."

"I was given to understand—" Dodd began.

"Herr Commander, the ultimate goal of the Nazi movement is not to benefit a self-serving astronaut who wishes to be king over one hundred some people in an otherwise populationless continent."

"I have plans, sir!"

"And so do we, Herr Commander Dodd. And so do we. At the moment, you are part of our plans. The knowledge within your computer banks, certain stored strategic items, these very craft themselves, all have their potential use to the Reich. The very existence of this base further saps the manpower of the rebellious forces under the command of Wolfgang Mann, an asset to our sacred movement in and of itself. You are obsessed with Akiro Kurinami. That you fear so greatly one obvious racial inferior speaks poorly for your manhood, Herr Commander. No. He shall die. But not at the expense of the greater purpose."

It sounded to Dodd as if part of Rausch's sentence was unfinished or missing and he hesitated to speak lest he inadvertently interrupt. When Rausch spoke no more for several seconds, Dodd asked, "Greater purpose? You mean your revolution."

"I mean evolution, Herr Commander. The survival of the fittest. Your Japanese nemesis will die if you are

41

correct that he will go to ground at the retreat of the bothersome Herr Doctor Rourke. But only because this fellow's death serves the greater purpose. See that you serve the greater purpose, Herr Commander. See to that if you value your life."

Christopher Dodd shivered. Rausch reminded him of the devil.

Chapter Four

Annie Rourke opened her eyes.

There was a grey half-light all about her, a hum so subtle she could not detect it at all unless she concentrated on it and nothing else.

The smell of disinfectant.

She closed her eyes . . . The gunship. The ocean. Otto injured. Natalia unable to function. From the pocket of the uncomfortable trousers she'd worn, she had taken the signaling device her father had given her, had called a transponder. For centuries, or so it seemed, she fought to stay afloat, to keep herself and Natalia and Otto afloat. And when it was finally ending, they had come. The man with the dark wavy hair, the wolfish smile, and the pretty dark eyes.

Into this— This.

She sat bolt upright, a restraint buckled loosely over her waist.

"Hi. Feeling better, Mrs. Rubenstein?"

She turned toward the reassuringly feminine voice. A light flickered on, like a small lamp, part of the bed in which Annie lay illuminated, the woman's face illuminated in it the next instant. Hair more brown than her own, what some called dark auburn, pretty

43

grey-green eyes like her mother, Sarah Rourke, had. A full, smiling mouth. She wore a white lab coat, and beneath it a khaki uniform shirt and matching khaki skirt. "You're, ah—"

"I'm Margaret Barrow, remember?"

"Doctor Barrow. I remember. How—"

"Why don't I save you the questions and I'll just give you the standard answers, okay?" Margaret Barrow smiled.

Annie laughed a little. "Okay."

"Fine. You're aboard the U.S.S. *Ronald Wilson Reagan,* the finest attack submarine in the Mid-Wake fleet. You've been asleep for about ten hours. Frankly, I thought you'd sleep longer than that. The man who was in charge of the team which pulled you out of the water is the Captain of this ship. He's Captain Jason Darkwood, just promoted while you were asleep, as a matter of fact, from Commander. Major Tiemerovna's condition is unchanged. Physically, I can say she is resting comfortably. Mentally, that's another question. Captain—ahh—Hammerschmidt right?"

"Right."

"His injuries weren't so severe as you might have feared. He won't be swimming any marathons for a little while, but he should be up and around soon enough. He's built tough, it appears. How do you like that for technical medical jargon, huh? Your father's a doctor. I was the one who first worked on him when they brought him in, Sam Aldridge is the black Marine Corps Captain. You met him."

"I remember. I remember Daddy telling me if it hadn't been for you he wouldn't have lived."

Margaret Barrow shrugged her shoulders and smiled. "Patients always say that kind of thing about doctors who administer emergency treatment. All I did was keep him breathing until the real pros at Mid-

44

Wake could take over. Your dad had the best. But he's a good guy. How's he doing?"

"I hope he's alive. He and my husband—they were trying—aww—" She felt a little light-headed.

"Hey, Mrs. Rubenstein," Doctor Barrow said, putting a hand gently against Annie's chest. "You're gonna wear yourself out and that's no good for anybody. Why don't you sleep a little more."

"Annie."

"What? Ohh—all right. I'm Maggie," and Margaret Barrow smiled and stuck out her right hand. Annie took her hand. It wasn't any kind of silly feminine handshake, but strong, like shaking hands with a man.

"Maggie. We've got to get in touch with my father and my husband. And the German authorities and—"

"Look, I just fix people. Communications isn't my department. But if you rest for a little while longer, I'll make sure Captain Darkwood gets down here to sick bay and then you can tell him. Everything's his department. Okay, Annie?"

Despite herself, Annie Rourke Rubenstein smiled, pushed her hair away from her face and neck, and leaned her head back on the pillow. She closed her eyes, but just to humor Maggie Barrow . . .

"I've plotted your course along the Izu Trench, Jason. We should be roughly off the coast of Iwo Jima within three hours traveling as we are."

Darkwood sipped at his coffee, tellling his First Officer, "Terrain following was the only way with the people we're carrying, Sebastian. If the Russians on the surface have any means of communicating with our underwater variety, everybody and his brother'd be looking for us by now. And if we stick to the volcanically active areas so we can mask our sonar

45

profile, well—"

"Every little bit helps," Sam Aldridge supplied.

"Right," Darkwood nodded.

"I'm gonna help myself to some more of your coffee," the Marine Captain announced, looking at Darkwood, then at Sebastian. "You want any more coffee, Mr. Sebastian?"

"No thank you, Captain Aldridge."

Aldridge shrugged his shoulders, saying, "I know what I want."

Darkwood checked the dual display, analog/digital Steinmetz on his left wrist. "You're still on duty, Sam. Come to think of it, we all are."

"If I may, Jason—why are we making our way toward Iwo Jima?" Sebastian asked.

"I hate to second Mr. Sebastian in anything, but that's a damn good question, Jason," Aldridge said. The coffee mug was steaming, and Aldridge set it down.

"I wish I could give you guys a damn good answer. But all I can say is that it's for a good reason. And, it'll take some of the heat off our backs a bit. Maybe. I'd tell you both if I could, but I'm under orders not to discuss Iwo Jima. So, I won't discuss it. Suffice it to say, if something were to happen to me, Sebastian, you'd find things concerning Iwo Jima in my safe. And, then—" And Darkwood grinned at his friend Sam Aldridge, "you could pester him, Sam."

"Hell of a lot I'd get outta him," Aldridge laughed, gesturing toward Sebastian.

Sebastian stood up, setting down his coffee cup, rubbing his hands together as if they were somehow cold. "I intend to pass by sick bay, to check on the health of our passengers. Is there any message you might like me to convey to Doctor Barrow?"

"Tell her I'll be there—" And he looked at his watch

again. "In an hour. Thanks."

"I gotta boogie, too, Jase," and Aldridge took one sip of his coffee, scowled, then followed Sebastian out.

Seeing T.J. Sebastian and Samuel Bennett Aldridge together was a relative rarity, unless the matter were duty related, one of the reasons Darkwood had his end-of-watch coffee sessions when circumstances allowed. One of the other reasons was that both men were his best friends and had been as long as he could remember.

The Sebastian-Aldridge "feud" (if it could be called that) was based on one of the incontrovertible facts of life in Mid-Wake: that the black community over the centuries of life beneath the sea had maintained much of its original racial integrity, hence had a restricted gene pool. The same could be said of many of the ethnic groups within Mid-Wake society, geneology a common passion and a necessity to avoid inadvertently close relatives from marrying. Someone had started it, that Sebastian and Aldridge were cousins. Sebastian was quiet, reserved, had an academic record which could have qualified him to teach at the Naval Academy. Aldridge was a wild and crazy Marine, although no less academically gifted.

And so had begun the feud or whatever it was, both men deeply respecting each other and each other's abilities, both men committed to the survival of Mid-Wake, but both men—and, in fairness, particularly Sebastian—resenting the insinuation that they were relatives to a degree which bordered occasionally on petulance and childishness.

The situation was abysmally stupid, Darkwood knew, but life frequently was.

Jason Darkwood set down his coffee cup, in the mood for something stronger as Aldridge had suggested. He crossed his cabin—which didn't take a great

47

deal of walking, since aboard a submarine space was always limited—and studied the map of the known world. It was a hologram, when viewed at one angle showing the world as it had been five centuries ago, before what Doctor Rourke called "the Night of the War," when viewed from the other angle showing the Earth as it appeared today to the best of the knowledge of Mid-Wake cartographers.

One of the fifty United States was all but gone, California its name, much of California fallen into the sea that night when the concussion from the bombings and missile strikes collectively shocked the geologic faultline and the tectonic plates separated. It was called the San Andreas fault; he remembered that from a history test he'd almost failed in grammar school. Part of Florida, where there had once been a peninsula, fell into the sea (no one knew the reason and it dawned on him that perhaps Doctor Rourke's daughter, now a passenger aboard the *Reagan,* might know). That took place sometime between the bombings and when the atmosphere ionized and most surface life had been destroyed.

Many islands had vanished below the surface, while some new ones had surfaced, perhaps really old ones which had sunk once before in the geologic epoch since the Earth began.

His eyes settled on an island which had neither risen nor sunk beneath the sea—Iwo Jima.

Iwo Jima was, of course, steeped in the history of World War Two, but whatever might have remained to remind the people of future years of this war had long since been washed away in the unprecedented tsunamis which had swept virtually every island and coastal area in the Pacific Basin when California fell into the sea.

Aboard the *Reagan,* Darkwood was the only person

48

who knew the current status of Iwo Jima as a top secret training facility for a group of men whose very existence was only rumor: The Special Warfare Group.

The Special Warfare Group, or "Gs" as they called themselves, consisted of volunteers from both the Navy and the Marine Corps, their training program accelerated since Mid-Wake's first encounter with the Rourke family, the reason for their inception that much more dramatized. For some time, under the leadership of Jacob Fellows, President of Mid-Wake, Admiral Rahn, Chief of Naval Operations, and General Gonzalez, Commandant of the Marine Corps, had quietly been siphoning away some of the very best men in both branches of service. Darkwood had originally learned of the program when General Gonzalez had tried to hire off Sam Aldridge, Aldridge originally tapped for one of the Gs' leadership positions, then lost to the Soviets during a commando raid on their submarine pens to gather intelligence on the unification of Soviet nuclear technology and their Island Class submarine fleet. Aldridge had been presumed dead. After helped to escape by John Rourke and the subsequent conclusion of Rourke's battle with the Soviet surface commander, Vladimir Karamatsov, Sam Aldridge was offered the job again, refusing, feeling he could do more as part of the corps rather than training for a war that was not yet to be fought.

And that was the crux of the issue from which the Gs had sprung: that a land war with Soviet forces might someday be inevitable and to prepare for that day a small group of highly trained special warfare personnel had to be ready to respond to the first wave, then form the nucleus around which a larger United States land force might be formed.

The Gs trained principally and were domiciled on Iwo Jima.

Without orders, he was proceeding there now. It would have been possible to work a radio relay through the system of communications buoys—perhaps—but such a radio message might well have been intercepted. From what little Annie Rubenstein had said when she was brought aboard, the land-based Soviet empire was embarked upon an offensive of unprecedented magnitude. If this were in some way connected to the Soviet forces beneath the waves which Darkwood and five centuries' worth of Americans from Mid-Wake had fought, the information was too valuable to risk sending to Mid-Wake by conventional means.

Yet, linking Iwo Jima to Mid-Wake was a laser optic cable, its security unquestionable, because to tamper with the cable's armoring would automatically sever the communications link.

He was violating security to preserve security.

The shape of Iwo Jima, as well as its size, had altered several times over the five centuries since the Night of the War. A large lagoon, deep enough for a careful submarine skipper to enter and exit, lay on the east side of the island.

The Gs' base was somewhere inland.

Finding it was the most expeditious means of notifying Mid-Wake of the Soviet surface offensive and querying Naval Operations concerning the possibilities of somehow contacting Doctor Rourke concerning Rourke's daughter's survival.

He tapped his finger against the holomap, then looked at his watch.

If he didn't want to be late for Margaret Barrow, he'd have to set a new speed record for paperwork.

Chapter Five

The Chairman's office was one of the few places where they could be alone, the invasion of the First City and the subsequent withdrawal of the Soviet Forces having turned everything upside down. But one thing never seemed to change, Sarah Rourke realized; that was her husband's sense of his ultimate rectitude. "John—"

"I love you and I don't want to lose you and the baby. What could be simpler than that?" He leaned against the Chairman's desk, lighting one of his cigars.

Sarah Rourke found herself trying to remember the first time she'd seen him smoke one of the noxious-smelling things. As far as cigars went, she supposed, his were better-smelling than most. But how men could—

"John. She's my daughter, too. And anyway, there's no place on Earth that's safe. We both know that. I mean, you should be happy; after all these years, I finally understand why you are the way you are. If something's right you do it and damn the consequences, personal or otherwise. And now that I understand that, agree with you philosophically, you try to turn it off."

"I'm glad you realize what you realize. I'm glad you feel as you do. But then you have to understand why I

51

feel as I do now. I don't see any rational reason why you should insert yourself and our unborn child into a situation so fraught with peril. I feel I know what's right, and as you implied, I should damn the consequences."

"So," she said to her husband, suddenly feeling tired, sitting on the arm of a black lacquer chair, "what you consider right is more right than what I consider right? That's ridiculous."

"You're going to have to abide by my decision because I feel it's right for all of us, not just you. I don't want anything to happen to you. Period."

She wondered if there were a blackly magical period of time for which she and her husband could be together, then at a precise, preordained moment go to each other's throats? But he never did that. He was always so calm, never fought. She fought. "Why did you make me pregnant?"

Sarah watched his brown eyes. There was no flicker of hesitation when he answered. "I wanted to make love to you. Sort of like you said a moment ago—damn the consequences. I'm glad you're pregnant."

She said it and felt guilty the moment she began to speak. "Now that I'm pregnant, fine—I can't do this, can't do that because of the welfare of the baby. Nuts. The baby's fine; I'm fine. You go off and play and—" She shut up.

"Hardly, Sarah," John Rourke told her, standing up, his attention seemingly riveted to the glowing orange tip of his cigar. "I haven't played in so long—" He let the sentence hang.

She crossed the room, despite the smell from his cigar put her arms around his neck. "I love you. I want to be with you."

His arms folded around her and she felt his breath against her cheek, her neck, her hair. "That was all I ever wanted. Don't you realize that after all this time?"

Sarah Rourke realized she hadn't and she kissed him hard on the mouth and he kissed her back and held her so tightly she thought she'd faint . . .

If gods had ever walked the Earth, John Rourke was their last true descendant, she realized. Michael was so much like him, and perhaps some woman had or someday would think the same of him and be just as right. Not gods as some profanity of divinity, but men who were above all others, perhaps touched in some special way with abilities and destinies to fulfill which were beyond normal mortals. She remembered Michael as helpless and fragile, so perhaps she could not quite see him as she saw her husband. But John, she was sure, had never been quite helpless, nor ever fragile. Had his mother yelled at him, complaining he hadn't cleaned his room or taken out the garbage? Had he ever neglected a responsibility, shirked a task?

It was hard to imagine him anything less than he was now.

He evidently concluded a quick discussion with the Chairman, then clasped the man's hand and walked on. She watched him. He was all in black, a combination of the Mid-Wake battle dress utilities and things from New Germany, black pants bloused over the tops of shiny black combat boots, a black knitted shirt open at the throat, a jacket of the same material as the pants, waist-length, fully open, a wide black leather belt, then a matching belt and gleaming black leather full flap holster slung at his right hip, his .44 Magnum revolver cased inside it.

He stopped, exchanged a few quick words with Colonel Mann, shook hands, walked toward her.

The helicopter's rotor blades sliced the air with a

steady, almost sensuous phutting sound.

He took her in his arms and she closed her eyes and pretended the moment would never end . . .

A second German helicopter gunship joined them, flying their "wing" until they crossed the open water to the far western side, a small German/Chinese base established there near where Vladmir Karamatsov had once set his field headquarters. There the gunship would be fitted with already waiting auxiliary fuel pods, additional armament, the floats which would allow it to land on the water's surface.

A German pilot was at the controls, Rourke taking the brief time this would afford him to rest. He would be the only pilot, but promised himself that he would teach Paul how to control the craft well enough that the younger man could keep it airborne.

John Rourke closed his eyes. Sleep would come, too soon end.

He could still see Sarah, beautiful-looking, ridiculous-looking in her BDUs and combat boots, see her looking after the gunship long after it was airborne. Eventually, he could no longer see her, knew she could see the gunship as only a dark speck on the horizon.

And he remembered the conversation he'd had with Michael when they'd horsebacked it to the ridge, come up behind the Mongols who had been waiting in ambush for Paul and María and Prokopiev and Han Lu Chen.

Michael had wanted frank answers concerning Natalia.

John Rourke had given his son no frank answers at all.

Rourke forced his eyes to stay closed. And in his mind he saw her eyes, the surreal blueness of them.

54

Would her eyes ever see the world as it really was again? Or was she destined to be a prisoner within her mind forever?

Rourke opened his eyes.

Conscious dreaming was something that ceased to exist after The Sleep. But there was always a chance that conscious dreaming might return.

And John Rourke knew the face that would be in his nightmare if he risked sleep. The gunship was surrounded by cloud cover now and John Rourke looked out of the helicopter, watching the wispy grayness. He thought of the line from Hamlet. He wondered if perhaps Shakespeare had once caused a woman great sorrow, too.

Chapter Six

Everywhere, gunships rose into the air, like gigantic black insects leaving some feast of carrion. Vassily Prokopiev reined in the Mongol horse he rode, the beast barely able to stand properly. "Why did I think that?" Prokopiev murmured under his breath, steam issuing from his lips as he exhaled.

Death.

It was the occupation he had trained for since boyhood. The heroic accounts of the Hero Marshal, Vladimir Karamatsov. The heroic struggle of the Hero Marshal against the evil forces of capitalism and the CIA assassin John Rourke. What was the CIA again? Was it not, in its way, like the KGB? Was the KGB intrinsically evil? Then was the CIA? John Rourke was not evil. Michael Rourke was a man to be counted on, trusted—a friend who had saved his life.

Few of the black machines were still on the ground in the valley stretching open before him, two of the lightweight armored personnel carriers forming a wedge at the mouth of the valley, guarding access. A huge bonfire roared to the north end of the valley, fuel explosions erupting from it, puffing upward. And he realized that damaged vehicles or equipment which could not be taken away were being burned. He began to dig in his heels, the animal shuddering under him.

Prokopiev dismounted, studied the horse's head for a moment. Weariness was in its eyes.

He set to uncinching the saddle, nearly bitten when he removed the bridle. The animal did not run off, merely stood. A feed bag was on the saddle which lay in the snow near Prokopiev's feet and he took the bag, slashed it open with a Chinese bayonet, then set it on the ground where the animal could bend to it easily. With the saddle blanket, he rubbed the animal down of its sweat. He was not a horseman, but realized that leaving the animal lathered in the freezing temperatures would not be good.

Having done all he could, he clapped the animal on the neck and strode down along the defile toward the valley entrance. Little remained of his uniform, little visible anyway beneath the Mongol outer garments he wore to keep warm. But these were his men, his Elite Corps. They would know him.

He cast aside the inferior bayonet. There were finely made Soviet knives available to officers of his rank and it would be easy enough to get hold of one, have the knife dispatched to him from the stores of such things held in reserve for the Elite Corps.

Prokopiev began to mentally review what he would tell the Comrade Colonel, who commanded the Armies of the Soviet now since the murder— Prokopiev stopped, the access hatches of one of the armored personnel carriers opening. He assumed he was recognized. John Rourke was not a murderer. Of course, the traitorous Major Tiemerovna, once wife of the Hero Marshal— She was the one who had murdered the Hero Marshal.

Prokopiev commenced again to walk.

It seemed as though there were two versions of the

truth, the one he had been told, the one he realized with his own senses. It was hard to imagine, for example, that Doctor Rourke, the father of Michael Rourke, would have criminally conspired with any woman to murder her husband.

Vassily Prokopiev realized that there was some error. After all, Comrade Colonel Antonovitch had not actually witnessed the slaying of the Hero Marshal. There was devious work afoot. Perhaps a conspiracy among those who had witnessed the Hero Marshal's death. It was impossible to imagine Doctor Rourke and this female Major, who was waiting in ambush for the Hero Marshal, giving him no chance to defend himself, murdering him when he surrendered for the sake of his men, then murdering his men as well.

The Comrade Colonel must be alerted to these discrepancies. Perhaps the entire new offensive was based on misinformation. The man Han Lu Chen by any standard was brave. The man Paul Rubenstein, a Jew, was heroic beyond measure. And, since he had first begun to learn, he had been told that Jews were at times capable of singular intellectual achievement but were a cowardly race, now exterminated. How then, unless the man Rubenstein was a racial anomoly, was this possible?

And would a man such as Doctor Rourke or Michael Rourke allow a daughter or sister to marry someone who was all but subhuman? Certainly not. Had other Jews been like Paul Rubenstein? And if they were, then why had he been taught what he had been taught?

No one would call out that he should halt, so Prokopiev halted of his own accord before the men guarding the valley entrance opened fire, as they would be under orders to do. "Comrades—it is Major Prokopiev! Do not shoot!"

He walked toward them with his hands outstretched, palms open.

This was a withdrawal, obviously. Because the Second Chinese City essentially no longer existed? Or had the plans for the offensive changed. "How goes the offensive, Comrades?"

If they told him what they thought was true, would it be true?

Chapter Seven

It was impossible to communicate with them effectively because they had no command of the language. He was able, by sheer force of concentration only, to make something from their words, searching for every possible similarity between their language and his, however remote or unlikely.

Bjorn Rolvaag sat up in bed and collected his thoughts while they merely watched him. Michael Rourke, Annie's brother, and the German woman, Doctor Maria Leuden, who was an archaeologist, mentioned Lydveldid Island, the Soviets (he mentally spat on them, individually and collectively), and performed ludicrous pantomimes of men fighting in battle.

It seemed likely that Lydveldid Island had been invaded.

He had asked about Annie Rubenstein and they had assumedly understood him well enough that they tried to answer. He got the impression—again by word association and through their pantomime—that Annie might be lost and in some danger. Somehow, he and Annie Rubenstein understood each other well enough that, despite words, the understanding was genuine, clear. And the Russian woman, Natalia Tiemerovna, the only one of them who could actually converse with him because she spoke so many languages so well that they made do and "talked"—the Russian woman with her pretty, sad blue eyes. Was she with Annie and lost, or lost and in danger on her own?

Bjorn Rolvaag could not be sure.

He watched their eyes watching his eyes.

He formed the few English words as carefully as he could for them so they would understand. "Rolvaag does go Lydveldid Island, Michael. Rolvaag does good." And he beat his fist against his own chest to demonstrate his hardiness. Adequate hardiness, his head still aching at times; but, he was confident that he was healing. Michael started to say something and, tired, Rolvaag merely repeated for them, "Rolvaag does go Lydveldid Island."

That should be clear enough for anyone to understand, he reasoned.

Chapter Eight

The Party Chairman entered the elevator and stood beside him, Antonovitch's eyes drawn to the Chairman's scientific advisor, Svetlana Alexsova. She was beyond pretty, more aptly described as beautiful, he thought, the blond hair so sternly arranged in a bun at the nape of her neck, the long, graceful neck, the mouth (devoid of lipstick) full and inviting. Her eyes, blue, were clear, purposeful, and when he heard her voice— "Comrade Chairman, the credit for the discovery belongs to Comrade Doctor Kulienkov. He is a young man, a member of my scientific team which has been developing the particle beam systems for military applications."

"Your leadership doubtlessly inspired Kulienkov, Comrade Doctor," Antonovitch blurted out, and she turned quickly and looked at him, the corners of her mouth dimpling with a quick, genuine-looking smile.

"Thank you Comrade Marshal."

He did not correct her, because he did not wish to. Technically, although he wore Colonel's rank, he was Chief Marshal of the Soviet Union. He supposed it was false modesty not to wear his proper rank, after all.

The elevator stopped. "How many floors, Comrade

Doctor, have we descended?"

As the doors opened, she answered him. "We are seven levels below the main level of the city, Comrade Marshal. This entire level is devoted to military research. For our testing purposes," she continued, the Chairman exiting the elevator, Antonovitch insisting that Doctor Alexsova exit ahead of him, "there is access to the summit of the mountain above by means of small conveyors and two large industrial lifts." She smiled again as she thrust her hands into the pockets of her white lab coat. The action accentuated the neatness of her figure. "It is quite the ride, Comrade Marshal, on the conveyors. More than a mile in total darkness except for the lights built into the belt itself, all within a seamless-appearing tube of transparent high density polymers, the tube inserted from the top of the bore hole, then heat welded by robotized track welders, their work controlled by remote video cameras. Quite the engineering marvel. As a scientist, I have always respected the skills of the engineer. Without such skills, science would be nothing more than a curiosity, a novelty. There could be no practical application."

They were walking along a gleaming corridor, a tunnel, Antonovitch imagined, at its farthest end a set of massive double doors. But parked along the corridor wall were three electric carts and Doctor Alexsova gestured toward one of them, the Comrade Chairman nodding, breaking the silence he'd begun when Antonovitch had first accompanied him from Party headquarters. "You told me, Comrade Marshal Antonovitch, that you need troops. Here, you will find that you will not need troops."

As they seated themselves in the cart, Doctor Alexsova at the controls, her dress shooting up to her thighs for an instant, Antonovitch quickly averted his eyes out of politeness, asked the Comrade Chairman,

"What is it that you intend to show me, Comrade Chairman?"

"The future of Soviet power."

Antonovitch turned and faced forward. He sat beside Doctor Alexsova and he savored the experience . . .

Beyond the double doors, at which security personnel were posted, lay a shorter corridor, set into the wall of the corridor a bank of elevators, at the corridor's end another set of double doors, electronic security here. Beyond these doors lay the laboratory complex, all one giant laboratory the size of some huge stadium, a kilometer square at least, the individual laboratories without any walls separating them for the most part. Doctor Alexsova spoke, addressing Antonovitch's unasked questions. "All personnel live on the level above us, complete educational, recreational, medical and cultural facilities at their disposal, Comrade Marshal. Their elevator keys only work in the second lift battery which you have seen between the sets of security doors. Without special authorization, they are not allowed beyond the second set of doors. It has been found that an atmosphere of scientific openness, where one team knows the work of the other, is best for rapid progress. Yet, the security difficulties such a system imposes are monumental. Hence, the system utilized here. You may have noticed a few of the laboratories are walled. This is not for secrecy, but for reasons related directly to the nature of the work."

The electric cart stopped near the center of the complex, the hum of equipment, whiffs of chemical odors, a hum of conversation all around him as he stepped down, offered to help Doctor Alexsova. She was already out of the cart.

65

The Comrade Chairman spoke, saying, "This is what I would never show to our so-called Hero Marshal, Comrade. He would have seen the work going on here and been obsessed with possessing it. Who knows whether spies brought him some information of this and it is for this reason he launched his so savage attack against the underground city with gas?"

"Then why do you show me this, Comrade Chairman?" Antonovitch's eyes riveted to the Chairman's impassive face, the drooping lids, drooping jowls, the impression almost of a face molded in wax and once partially melted.

"I have no choice, Antonovitch. You wish peace through victory. You wish to avoid the use of nuclear weapons. And so do I. Here is the way."

Doctor Alexsova waited a respectful distance away, the Comrade Chairman's face brightening as he turned toward her. "Show him everything. I shall be waiting in your office, Comrade Doctor."

"Yes, Comrade Chairman," she nodded.

As the Comrade Chairman climbed back into the electric cart, then drove off, Antonovitch watched after him, after a moment feeling Doctor Alexsova at his side. "Much work has been done here, Comrade Marshal. It is now at your disposal to lead the forces of the Soviet people to victory, to our finest hour."

Antonovitch turned and looked at her. "Yes, Comrade Doctor." He was reminded of the Judeo-Christian myth concerning the Garden of Eden. He wondered vaguely whether the Comrade Chairman or the beautiful Comrade Doctor had the role of the snake. Because he was about to be given all the forbidden fruit he could ever want, he realized . . .

Yuri Kulienkov was indeed quite young. No more

than twenty-five. As he powered up his apparatus, he spoke. "I have a considerable difficulty, Comrade Marshal, talking about things in a way that is not scientific. I apologize, Comrade Marshal."

"You have nothing to apologize for, Comrade Doctor Kulienkov. Genius requires no apology. I will confess that I know very little of science," Antonovitch told him. He caught the reaction in Doctor Alexsova's eyes. Favorable.

Kulienkov cleared his throat. He was a skinny man, the ravages of adolescence still visible in a few pockmarks on his cheeks and forehead, shoulders hunched beneath his lab coat as he bent over something that looked like a combination of a gun and a radio set at the side of a huge fish tank. Had signals been crossed and was Kulienkov showing him something to do with the advancements in particle beam weaponry? "This came about by accident, Comrade Marshal," Kulienkov began. "And without Comrade Doctor Alexsova's policy of openness it would never have been possible." He looked over his shoulder and smiled at her, his glasses slipping a little, dark hair in his eyes. Did Kulienkov have a crush on his superior?

Doctor Alexsova smiled back at him. "Thank you, Kulienkov."

Kulienkov began to speak again. "I knew, of course, that there was an important project concerning communications under the sea. I knew that various frequency ranges were being tried and that conventional laser systems could be utilized but only as part of an already established system of links. So, I asked myself how it might be if a conventional laser were to ride on a particle beam as a carrier? The heat generated by the particle beam would evaporate the water surrounding it and the laser beam would not be dispersed any more in the water than it would be in the air. So, I tried it. Here it is."

The buzzing sound Antonovitch had been aware of for several seconds suddenly became louder. Involuntarily, he stepped back across the floor of the laboratory, away from the now-glowing apparatus. "It was simple once the theory was developed, really. This is simply a much modified form of the plasma energized particle beam system developed for armored vehicles."

Antonovitch looked at Doctor Alexsova. "A particle beam weapon that does not require something the size of a mountain for its energy source?"

She smiled, said nothing. Kulienkov was still talking. ". . . is merely a matter of firing it—at reduced charge levels of course—and aiming the laser beam wherever one wishes to. Like this." Kulienkov began whispering into a microphone as he flipped a switch.

And there was a loud buzzing sound.

The water along the center of the tank seemed to instantly boil—but in a straight line. Steam rose from the tank in a huge cloud. At the far end of the tank was a conventional-seeming speaker. From it came the voice of Kulienkov, amplified to stentorian volume. ". . . to his ability, to each according to his needs."

Marx.

But Antonovitch was reminded more of Buck Rogers.

Chapter Nine

"Now that we will be able to communicate through the water successfully, it will be possible to recontact Soviet forces under the sea. The technological breakthroughs which have so fortuitously come about have enabled us to pursue the alliance and, if necessary, should no alliance result, will enable us to vanquish these forces should such become necessary." The Comrade Chairman smoked a cigarette, leaned back in Doctor Alexsova's chair, placed his feet on her desk. Had he been smoking a fat cigar, he would have made the perfect caricature of the rich Capitalist, Antonovitch thought.

Doctor Alexsova had been excluded from this meeting, and only the two of them sat in the soundproof office. Antonovitch could hear the sucking sounds as the Comrade Chairman would inhale on his cigarette, hear them clearly with the almost total absence of background noise. Except for the hiss of air through two air-conditioning vents, there was no noise except for their breathing and the sounds from the Comrade Chairman's cigarette. The sucking sound alternated with a faint crackling sound, the tobacco burning.

The Comrade Chairman continued speaking. "I am reminded of the so-called 'SETI' programs I have read of."

"Search for Extra-Terrestrial Intelligence," Antonovitch said without thinking.

"Yes, Comrade Marshal," as if to say, remember I am the Comrade Chairman and I should not be interrupted. "These SETI programs fired radio signals into the void of the cosmos. We will fire signals into the void of the deep." Antonovitch didn't really consider the ocean a void, in fact just the opposite, but refrained from correcting the Comrade Chairman. "And, since we know the approximate area in which to search, it should be a matter of days, a few weeks at the most before contact is made."

"Forgive me, Comrade Chairman, but what if our Soviet brothers beneath the ocean's surface do not choose to respond?"

"The message," the Comrade Chairman smiled," will be such that they will have no choice. I intend to inform them that there is a substantial possibility that, if they do not act at once, the Germans, who are allies of our other enemies, will launch a nuclear missile which will so totally destroy the atmosphere that their precious ocean will be vaporized around them."

Antonovitch leaned forward, sitting at the edge of his chair. "But, Comrade Chairman—"

"I am merely extrapolating from the facts. Your own high altitude surveillance confirms that it is likely the Germans are perfecting a nuclear warhead to possibly use against us. You must admit," and his drooping, wrinkled face for once smiled, "they will be intrigued by this message, our Soviet brothers. Hmm?"

"Yes, Comrade Chairman," Antonovitch nodded.

"So. If we can forge an alliance, so be it. If not, we shall destroy them with our particle beam weapons.

Once they respond, we shall know their exact location beneath the ocean surface, each signal computer monitored, of course." And he smiled again, stubbing out his cigarette as he shifted his feet from the corner of the desk and looked Antonovitch in the eye. "We have become invincible, Comrade Marshal."

"Yes—invincible."

Chapter Ten

The composite video display which dominated the forward bulkhead was set for forward view and revealed shoaling some five hundred yards ahead of the *Reagan* along its present course. Sebastian's long fingers were splayed across the illuminated plotting board which dominated the control station.

"Navigation—ten degrees left rudder and hold it there."

Lieutenant Junior Grade Lureen Bowman responded "shifting to ten degrees left rudder, Captain."

Darkwood swung his chair right. "Communications—are you picking up anything, Lieutenant?"

"Just some low frequency noise, Captain. It could be electronic stuff that's out of tune and crept into the wrong bands. I can't make anything out of it at all, sir."

"Very good, Lieutenant Mott. Advise me if there's any change."

"Aye, sir."

Darkwood rotated his chair to face forward again, the shoaling more pronounced now on the video display.

"Bring that rudder amidships again, Navigator." He refused to call a woman "Helmsman" or, worse still, "Helmsperson."

Sebastian spoke. "Captain, I'd advise blowing fifteen percent air to the starboard tanks."

Darkwood's eyes flickered from the video screen to T.J. Sebastian's face. "Order the blow, Mr. Sebastian, and alert the crew we'll be running out of trim."

"Aye, Captain, blowing fifteen percent negative buoyance starboard tanks." Sebastian reached for his microphone, speaking into it. "Now hear this. This is the First Officer speaking. Until further notice, secure to run fifteen percent off trim to port." Sebastian put down the microphone and ordered Lieutenant Bowman, "Navigation. Blow fifteen percent air to starboard tanks and hold." Sebastian turned to the Engineering Station saying, "Commander Hartnett, please advise me should there be any change in reactor status."

Hartnett nodded, saying, "I will advise you, Mr. Sebastian."

Darkwood's command chair was gyroscopically balanced, and automatically adjusted fifteen degrees of attitude toward starboard. He had been to Iwo Jima once before for one of the few surface survival classes, this more years ago than he had wanted to remember when he had been a student at the Naval Academy. He had been one of five cadets allowed to stand on the bridge while the skipper of the submarine which had brought them there navigated the inlet. There were charts of course which showed the depths and bottom contours but it was a matter of pride in the submarine service that you didn't scrape the bottom with your hull. Plus, since this was an unauthorized, unannounced visit to the island, there was always the possibility that some overzealous person working with the island defenses might shoot first and ask questions afterward. "Lieutenant Mott."

74

"Aye, Captain?"

"Send this for me on all standard defense frequencies using the Sigma Three Code. Compliments to Colonel P.Q. Armbruster, Commanding. This is the United States attack submarine *Ronald Wilson Reagan.* We are entering through the inlet without orders because of an emergency security situation. We will surface at the approximate center of the lagoon—" and he checked the face of the dual display Steinmetz on his left wrist. "We will surface at the approximate center of the lagoon at precisely 0900 hours. I anticipate he will have security personnel in the vicinity to verify identification. Signed Darkwood, Captain, Commanding U.S.S. *Reagan.* If you got it all, there's no need to read it back, Andy."

"Aye, sir. I got it."

"Send at once, Lieutenant." And Darkwood turned away. The video display's forward view revealed that the shoaling was receding to starboard. "Mr. Sebastian. Correct this uncomfortable list to port. I think we're safe enough now if we surface to periscope depth and resume normal speed while keeping a good eye on the bottom."

"Aye, Captain. Navigation. Equalize the blow. Bring us up to periscope depth and adjust present speed to all ahead two-thirds."

"Aye, Mr. Sebastian. Adjusting to periscope depth."

"Maintain present course, Mr. Sebastian—unless you see fit to do otherwise."

"Aye, Captain. Maintaining present course and speed." Sebastian picked up his microphone again. "This is the First Officer speaking. Secure from the previously mentioned navigational correction."

Jason Darkwood just looked at his First Officer as he stood. He'd never heard one like that before. He moved aft, Seaman First Class Tagachi at the periscope controls. "Morris, run her up for me when we reach periscope depth."

"Aye, Captain. We gonna breathe real air, Captain?"

"Shore leave? If we have the time, I suppose. But I understand breathing real air can be hazardous to your health. I had a cough for days afterward the last time I did."

"Really, sir?"

"Right," Darkwood grinned, clapping Tagachi on the shoulder, laughing.

Navigation announced periscope depth, Sebastian echoing it, Morris Tagachi activating the periscope controls.

Darkwood stepped to the periscope, the handles lowering. Each time he used either this or the attack periscope, he unfailingly thought of the centuries-old movies he had seen of the early days of submarining. The slightly grizzled, stubble-faced captain ordered, "Up periscope!" and snapped down the handles from the dully gleaming brass tube, his face sweating as he crouched to peer through the tube.

With the periscope aboard the *Reagan,* there was no need to crouch because they were adjustable to various height levels instantly. There was no reason to sweat unless one was working out in the gymnasium (granted, it wasn't that large). Wearing a beard as long as it was in Regs was acceptable, but never stubble. He'd always secretly wondered how the Navy Department expected someone to grow a beard within Regs without growing through the stubble stage first.

He worked the buttons for focus as he looked into the periscope, surveying the lagoon which they were now entering. He felt almost like Captain Nemo returning to the island that was the seat of his anguish, but on this island were fellow officers and men in the service of Mid-Wake, fellow Americans.

And—

"Sebastian! Battle Stations! Get us out of here! Now! Down periscope!"

Darkwood pushed past Seaman First Tagachi, sprinting toward the Command Chair, taking the three steps down to the Control and Navigation level in a jump, the *Reagan* already beginning to rock under him the instant Sebastian ordered, "Now hear this. Now hear this. Battle stations. I repeat, Battle Stations. This is not a drill." The Klaxon sounded. Sebastian threw down the microphone, ordering, "Navigator, hard right rudder. All back. Blow air. Engineering—reactor status. Navigator—bring her about—faster. Engineering—that reactor status."

Saul Hartnett sang out, "Both port and starboard reactors on line and running smooth, Mr. Sebastian."

Darkwood stared at the video display as though he were looking through some huge window. On the beach, at the far side of the lagoon, he had seen Russian troops but no sign of their submarine, and that was what frightened him. Darkwood called back, "Navigator—are we about yet?"

"We're coming about now, Captain, in five . . . four . . . three . . . two . . . one . . . We are about, Captain."

"Rudder amidships, bring us to half flank speed." Darkwood moved to the illuminated plotting table beside Sebastian. "Communications—bring up aft projection on the screen."

"Aye, Captain—you have aft projection."

Darkwood turned toward the screen, the picture changed instantly. There was nothing suspicious within visual range. "Communications—give me split screen imaging fore and aft."

"Split screen imaging now, Captain, as indicated."

The video display was now evenly divided between

fore and aft views and, to prevent a panicked Captain from making some critical mistake, the words "fore" and "aft" flashed on and off on their appropriate screens. Darkwood focused his attention on the illuminated plotting board. The *Reagan* was into the inlet channel. Sebastian had done his work well and so had the Navigator, Lureen Bowman. Darkwood made a mental note to mention this in the log. Without looking up, he called to Saul Hartnett. "Engineering—be ready for overdrive as soon as we clear the channel."

"Aye, Captain," Hartnett sang back.

They were entering the portion of the channel where the shoaling had been. "Navigation—give me a slow blow to seventy percent negative buoyancy on portside tanks and eighty-five percent on starboard proportionately, and be ready to terminate the blow on my signal."

"Aye, Captain, starting the blow now."

It suddenly dawned on Darkwood, as things did at the most ridiculous times, that it was almost crude carrying on such rapid-fire buoyancy orders with a female helmsman. "Warfare."

"Aye, Captain," Lieutenant Louise Walenski called back.

"Torpedo tubes fore and aft loaded and operational with HEIS, Captain."

"Stand by, Walenski. Communications—get on the usual Soviet operational frequencies."

Andrew Mott called back, "I am already monitoring, Captain. If they've seen us, nobody's talking about it. Who's out there Captain?"

Darkwood grabbed Sebastian's microphone from the hanger over the table. "This is the Captain speaking. The island of Iwo Jima is supposed to be a top secret American training center for surface warfare operations. While approaching the island just upon entering the lagoon, I viewed a significant force of personnel in Soviet Marine Spetznas uniforms and full battle gear. This could have been an exercise utilizing enemy uniforms and equipment. On that off chance, I elected to run. If it isn't, we're in potentially deep shit because they wouldn't be here without one of their Island Classers and we all know how much fun Island Classers can be, right? So stand by. I'll keep you informed. And keep sharp at those battle stations." He racked the microphone and called to Lieutenant Kelly, "Sonar—anything I should worry about?"

"Not yet, Captain," she called back.

"Keep me informed."

"Aye, Captain."

He'd made a critical tactical error—something he also intended to note in his log in the hopes of preventing some other Captain from doing the same thing someday. Pulling into an American base, assuming only American personnel would be monitoring his short range communications. Communications—"Communications—anything?"

"Not a word, Captain."

"Keep monitoring." They were listing again and the deck didn't compensate like his chair did. As he eyed the split video image, he said to Sebastian, "If you have any brilliant insights, Commander Sebastian, now's not the time to hold off on mentioning them."

"Captain, it seems to me that an analysis of the details suggests why we have not been picked up. If an Island Class submarine isn't waiting for us when we exit the channel, my theory will likely be correct."

"Do we have to use that as the acid test?"

"It would appear that either indeed the personnel you saw in Marine Spetznas black were merely engaged in a realistic training exercise, in which case we will merely be late for our rendezvous, or, more likely, since Lieutenant Mott has not received a reply to your Sigma code greeting, there was no one to receive it or everyone was too busy to respond or in fear of their own communications being monitored. Which leads me to infer that the island is under attack. There is ample supporting evidence, however circumstantial, to support such a hypothesis. Marine Spetznas communications equipment of standard issue type of which we are aware is not designed to nor is it ordinarily capable of intercepting short range signals in the range used by our submarines. If an Island Class submarine were surfaced or submerged on the opposite side of an island of the general topographical configuration of Iwo Jima, it is doubtful in the extreme that the said vessel would have intercepted our communications or our running noise, Captain."

"Then they don't know we're here!"

"Unless an Island Class vessel is waiting for us, that seems reasonable to assume based on current data."

"Did I ever tell you I love you?" And Darkwood clapped Sebastian on the back. He pulled down the microphone again. "This is the Captain speaking. Captain Aldridge and Lieutenant Stanhope to the bridge on the double." He looked at Sebastian as he racked the microphone. "If you're right, we're going to have to play this close to the vest, Sebastian. What's the nearest American vessel you know of?"

"Commander Pilgrim's ship, the *Wayne*, Captain."

Darkwood nodded. Walter Pilgrim was a good man under fire and the *John Wayne* was a good vessel. "All right—we can't risk trying to contact the *Wayne*—yet. Plot their approximate position as soon as we're out of here and in deep water, then update the plot so we'll have an idea how close some assistance might be if it gets that far."

They were nearly out of the channel, the shoaling

gone. "Navigator. Right the helm."

"Aye, Captain, righting the helm."

His fingers were too busy at the plotting table to keep them crossed, but they were crossed in spirit . . .

"I can help you. My mother had volunteer nursing experience before the war and she's had a hell of a lot since, my father's a doctor and I'm not half bad at First Aid."

"All right," Margaret Barrow told her, Annie Rourke Rubenstein belting a lab coat over her hospital gown with a little over two feet of dental floss. "Can you check syringes? They're like the ones in your day, more or less."

"I'll fake it," Annie told her, muttering, "Your day" under her breath, going to the cabinet Margaret Barrow gestured toward. Annie Rubenstein realized, of course, that she was a living breathing walking and talking anachronism.

"And first chance you get, in my office I've got some extra clothes—just in case there's a bleeder and I zig when I should have zagged. Just take the rank insignia off the collar, okay?"

"Okay." She began to check the syringes.

Chapter Eleven

Darkwood sat in his command chair. There had been no Island Class Submarine waiting for them and they were hiding now well off the coast of Iwo Jima in deep water, still at Battle Stations.

In a ragged semicircle between his chair and the steps stood Sam Aldridge, Tom Stanhope, and Sebastian. "I'm betting Sebastian's right, gentlemen. That means we've got a bunch of our GIs in shit up to their elbows back there on Iwo Jima. And aboard the *Reagan* we've got Doctor Rourke's daughter, a German officer, and Major Tiemerovna, the two women certainly potential bargaining chips our garden variety Soviet enemies could use as a wedge with the Soviet forces on the surface. An alliance like that could mean the end for all of us. There's one clear course of action. And that's our only chance. Sebastian?"

"Yes, Jason."

"You'll take the *Reagan* and make best speed toward Mid-Wake. Once you're out of range of the Island Classer our Marine Spetznas friends came from, attempt to contact the *Wayne*. Notify them of the situation and ask them to come to our aid. Mr. Stanhope—"

"Sir!"

"Lieutenant—you'll be in charge of security aboard the *Reagan* and that means looking after our passengers. If anything happens, they go before the women and children. Got me?"

"Yes, sir."

"Good. Sam. You and I are taking the majority of the Marine Security detail and heading for Iwo Jima. No sense attacking some damned Island Classer with bare hands and Bowie knives. We hit the side of the island where the lagoon is, on the assumption that some of our guys are still going to be operational. The plan's loose, but the crux of the whole thing is that we win. You can fill in the blanks however you wish."

"Gee whiz, Jase."

"Yeah—I knew you'd love it." And Darkwood looked at Sebastian. "I'll expect you back here for us as quick as you can get our charges to Mid-Wake. And don't forget about helping Mrs. Rubenstein to contact her father and her husband. There's got to be some way of doing it. And knowing Doctor Rourke, he'll be looking for her and for Major Tiemerovna."

"Yes, Captain."

"I'll want you to get us within range of the island. I'm officially transfering to you temporary command of the *Reagan* as of—" And Darkwood looked at the Steinmetz. "As of 0952 hours, and Captain Aldridge and Lieutenant Stanhope witness that and I'll make certain the log reflects that. God Bless us all."

"Amen to that," Sam Aldridge grunted.

Chapter Twelve

Her office was at once Spartan and luxurious, elegant in its austerity. The desk was unadorned, but was of real wood, something almost impossible to obtain within the underground city. The wristwatch she wore was of the most expensive brand. Her clothes, tailored, functional, also of the finest fabrics. He had known many women of the Underground City. This one dressed like the mistress of a commissar.

"This is the original prototype of the plasma-powered particle beam gun. It has been successfully tested on armored vehicles, helicopters, and bipod mounted as a replacement for the conventional caseless machine gun in the current inventory."

She was beautiful. Nicolai Antonovitch was having a hard time concentrating on anything else but that fact. "How many and how fast, Comrade Doctor Alexsova?"

"At present, Comrade Marshal, the weapons must be calibrated by hand and this requires considerable testing. Should one of these overload, it will, of course, explode. We have approximately one hundred of the weapons in operational order, none of these the model designed to replace the machine gun. The power packs are still a difficulty, but my people are working on it in three shifts throughout each twenty-four-hour period. The solution is forthcoming, I assure you. More of the weapons are being produced daily, and the calibration process is even now being streamlined to meet full production needs."

He recalled the Americanism about clouds with silver linings. Here was the opposite case, certainly. "These one hundred weapons which are available to mount on helicopters and armored vehicles. They are fully operational and can be relied upon thoroughly?"

"That is the only way they leave here, Comrade Marshal. I have full confidence in them."

"Where are they?" Antonovitch asked her.

"Ready for you to examine, Comrade Marshal."

"Tonight?"

"If—if you wish," and she averted her eyes.

He had known Karamatsov long enough to recognize deceit and treachery. He knew she was practicing both and decided he would enjoy it. "Tell me, Comrade Doctor. Just how deep are your feelings— loyalty to the State?"

"There is nothing I would not do, Comrade Marshal."

"Svetlana—it is one of the most beautiful of names for a woman. May I call you by your first name—of course, only when we are alone?"

"I am honored, Comrade Marshal."

He doubted the chief science advisor to the Soviet government was all that terribly honored at the prospect of having a soldier's boots beside her bed. He was being courted, and not by Svetlana Alexsova. He reached out his right hand and closed it over her hand. "Svetlana. Your beauty has captivated me. But, you must know that. I must be obvious."

"Comrade Marshal—I—"

"You are overwhelmed," he nodded, smiling. It was evident that the Chairman wanted him happy, wanted him eager to serve the Soviet interest. And Comrade Doctor Alexsova was to ensure that loyalty, that enthusiasm.

There was no need to provide him with some added incentive to serve the Soviet people. It was his life. He smiled. Comrade Doctor Svetlana Alexsova did not know that. And she, too, was willing to serve the Soviet interest. "You have captured my heart, Svetlana. It is very hard, out there, fighting constantly. One loses sight of what ordinary humanity must be like. The loneliness is intolerable." He had used that speech several times in the past, and often wondered why some intelligent woman did not simply laugh at him when he used it. Certainly this woman should laugh. She did not. "I want to possess you, Svetlana."

"Yes, Comrade Marshal."

He stood, walked to her desk. She stood. She took a step nearer to him. There was little choice, really. Should he not attempt to seduce her, the Comrade Chairman might suspect disloyalty or homosexuality, in either case disaster. And she was so very beautiful.

He did not ask if she had a health certificate. She obviously did as did he. "Do you—ahh—do you stay where the other scientists stay, Svetlana?"

"I have a room there, of course, but I find my apartment in the city more conducive to thought."

"Umm—I would like to see it very much. Might I do that? See it?"

"Yes, Comrade Marshal."

"Nicolai, Svetlana—Nicolai," and he held her hand more tightly. The late-morning meetings would have to wait, as would be expected.

Chapter Thirteen

The cloud cover remained unbroken as John Rourke piloted the German gunship over the Daito Islands, almost a border line between the East China Sea and the Philippine Sea, toward the Tropic of Cancer. Paul Rubenstein sat beside him. Rourke's eyes flickered over the horizon indicator. They were in level flight, but visually it was hard to be certain, the gray of the sky and the gray of the sea blending unnervingly in an effect that made them seem one.

It should have been warm here, but the outside cabin temperature at the comparatively low altitude at which they flew was below freezing. Wind-tossed whitecaps formed the only relief from the gray monotony surrounding them, the only possible means of sensual orientation for up and down. In the interests of not attracting Soviet attention, Rourke elected not to send out constant signals which might be picked up by Mid-Wake vessels because they might also be picked up by the Russians. But such radio silence caution didn't preclude listening.

The cacophony of natural radio emissions coming through the headsets they both wore was maddening,

Paul Rubenstein saying over the whir of the rotor blades, "I'm getting a headache listening to this stuff. And to think all of this is natural radio emission. Wild."

Paul had been starting fragmentary conversations ever since he'd come out of his sleep period, John Rourke not yet taking his. He'd taught Paul in the first few hours how to hold the machine on course at altitude, which was enough to allow Rourke to catch a few hours' rest. He did not look forward to rest, because it was inactivity and there was too much to do. Paul spoke out of nervousness over the fate of his wife, Rourke's daughter, Rourke knew. And he tried to keep the conversations going because he, too, was frightened that Annie, and Natalia and Otto Hammerschmidt as well, might be lost.

"That explosive device we have. You sure they'll pick it up?"

"If we detonate it directly over Mid-Wake," Rourke nodded, "they'll pick it up. Might even send a submarine up to investigate. They'd better or we're out of luck. Once we're over the Bonin Trench, I'll tack us almost due south toward the Marianas. That way, we can set her down and do any last-minute checks before we strike out for the open sea between Midway and Wake Islands. Be good to stretch our legs, too."

"You're counting on the Americans at Mid-Wake having picked up that transponder signal, aren't you?" Paul Rubenstein said suddenly.

"I have to. Otherwise, Annie and Natalie and Otto are—"

"Yeah," the younger man said, looking away to starboard. "They're dead. Shit. I mean—"

"Why were you and Annie and all the rest of us born into this?"

"Yeah. This weather—I mean—and the Soviets trying to get the Chinese missiles, all of this—I mean, isn't the world fucked up enough? It should be spring. It's winter. This should be the tropics. It looks like the Arctic down there. What if we so screwed up the world that it's never going to go back to normal?"

"'Normal' is a very subjective term," John Rourke observed. "What was normal during the last decades of the twentieth century isn't necessarily always normal. The Earth has endured a significant number of climatic variations more bizarre than this, probably." If Paul retreated from the reality of the single option theory— that Annie and the others were dead if they had not been taken in by one of the submarines of Mid-Wake— John Rourke realized that so did he. If Paul chattered, he found some intellectual triviality and played with it.

"If she's dead, John—if she's—if she is, I'd never marry again. And, so help me God, I'll find every one of Antonovitch's troops and kill them—hunt down the last damn one and choke the life out of him."

"What happened to 'Vengeance is mine, sayeth the Lord'?"

"What happened to justice, John?"

John Rourke had no answer for that . . .

The snow was still falling. Akiro Kurinami had built a fire to keep from freezing, but built it beneath a rocky overhang, keeping the fire as low and smokeless as possible. Periodically, Soviet helicopters still moved through the gray skies overhead.

As best he could judge, if he could begin to press on within the next hour or so, he would reach Doctor Rourke's Retreat sometime between dusk and dawn. Once inside, he could contact the Germans outside

Eden Base. And he could turn on John Rourke's water heating system and indulge himself for as long as he wished in the warm water, borrow clothes that were dry and warm, make a meal for himself that was warm.

He rubbed his hands over his modest fire, trying to imagine what warm would be like again.

Chapter Fourteen

He had been learning how to fly the J7-Vs, taking each opportunity he could at the yoke, and he "flew" one now. He hadn't taken it airborne, nor would he land it, although in a pinch he was confident he could do either, had done both under the watchful eye of various of the German pilots, with the permission of Colonel Wolfgang Mann. Oddly now, Mann was one of the passengers aboard the J7-V, along with Michael's mother and Maria Leuden and Bjorn Rolvaag and a small unit of German commandos.

The J7-V Michael Rourke flew was one of eighteen J7-Vs, the largest group of these planes Michael had ever seen assembled, which flew a Polar route toward the conflict in Lydveldid Island. Colonel Mann was following his father's advice concerning bottling up the Soviet Forces in Hekla, then proceeding to throw everything available against the Soviet offensive at Eden Base, but following John Rourke's plan with a twist. Bjorn Rolvaag, from what little Michael and Maria Leuden had been able to understand, was obsessed with returning to Iceland because his native land was in danger. From everything Michael Rourke had ever read, the Scandinavian people as a whole were fiercely patriotic and the Icelandics, of course, were descendants of the Scandinavians, of the Viking explorers.

At Rolvaag's feet sat his dog, Hrothgar, the animal more quiet than his master, sleeping peacefully. Michael had wondered, been unable to ask, if the dog could "hold it" long enough to make the journey. From the First City, they had traveled northeastward over the Sea of Japan and to the Sea of Okhotsk, landing in a remote waste in Northeastern Siberia to make a last-minute check before crossing the Pole. Hrothgar had relieved himself, then returned to stay by his master's side, Rolvaag looking almost invigorated by the very sight of the barren arctic wilderness. Maria had stood outside, huddling beside him—Michael Rourke—and Sarah Rourke had stayed inside the fuselage deep in conversation with Wolfgang Mann.

Then airborne again, making the jump over the Pole to Greenland.

The twist to John Rourke's plan was a simple one. Colonel Mann, taking Michael's mother with him because she and the unborn child she carried would be safer with his force, would travel to Eden Base. But Michael and Maria (although Michael had protested, she had insisted and he had agreed she could stay with him) would join Bjorn Rolvaag and a small group of German commando volunteers in an attempt to penetrate the Hekla community, rescue Madame Jokli, the Icelandic President, and generally do as much damage to the Soviet military position as possible.

The J7-V cruised comfortably, easily beneath his hands and Michael Rourke used the time to survey what lay beneath him. Vast ice fields, as far as the eye could see in any direction. The German maps of the

94

area showed the previous known boundary of the Ice Cap. Its volume had increased dramatically. Was the Earth entering a new Ice Age?

Or was it entering the last age?

If they met with success in Iceland and Colonel Mann met with success in Georgia at Eden Base, would the war which had lasted for five centuries be closer to conclusion? Or, would the Russians redouble their efforts to gain control of Chinese nuclear warheads and simply use them out of desperation or sheer evil stupidity?

Some scientific opinion was that one more nuclear detonation would end everything forever.

He took his eyes from the ice fields and his instruments and looked back along the interior of the fuselage. Maria Leuden slept in one of the chairs, seatbelted in, head cuddled against the bulkhead, a blanket drawn up to her chin. He loved her, as much as he had loved Madison—still loved Madison—but differently, not more, not less. It would have been nice to say to her, "Marry me and I'll take you away from all of this. We can have children and they'll be able to grow up in a peaceful world full of opportunity." But had anyone ever been able to truthfully say that? Had there ever been peace? And opportunity, he had always been taught, always believed, was made, not just there, waiting to be snatched.

They were man and wife in every way, really. They slept together. She scrubbed his back in the shower, cut his hair for him, cared for him. He would give his life to protect her and she would do the same for him.

Would there ever even be the time to ask her to marry him? Was his father right? Sometimes he could close his eyes and see Madison, see her swollen abdomen and the child there. Would the baby have been

95

a boy or a girl? And, sometimes, too, he could see the snow-covered mound beneath which she and the baby lay now, Madison wearing her wedding dress.

Michael Rourke realized he was biting his lower lip and there was a tightness in his throat. He forced himself to run an unnecessary instrument check.

Chapter Fifteen

Jason Darkwood broke atmosphere, shaking his head to clear it. Breaking atmosphere, as the Russians called it, was never a pleasant sensation.

One thing that doubtlessly the people of Mid-Wake and their Soviet counterparts held in common was physical addiction to the scrubbed and oxygen-rich artificial environment into which they were born, in which they grew, worked, played (presumably the Soviets played), and lived and eventually died. As a submariner, there was really little difference, the atmosphere content aboard any vessel basically identical to that within the domes beneath the sea. But, as a submariner, or a Marine, there was always the possibility of actually breaking atmosphere, coming out of the sea into the oxygen-depleted surface atmosphere. The shock to the body was momentarily overwhelming.

Civilians, who never left the domes throughout their entire lives unless involved in some scientific activity, imagined the fresh air of the surface to be unimaginably sweet. Indeed, there were breezes which cooled the skin, invigorated it, but no more so than the water would.

Darkwood often wondered if it would be worth it to ever return to the surface, to live on the land. Beneath the sea, in the moments when thoughts of warfare could be pushed aside, it was very beautiful, clean, rich. The surface was a desert, a cold and inhospitable environment in which oxygen deprivation was so normal that no one noticed it, if the Rourkes were any way typical. Portions of the surface were still so highly radioactive that they could not be entered, might never be able to be entered again.

And yet, at Mid-Wake, there were growing numbers, among the young people especially, who demanded a return to the surface, insisted that they were being manipulated by the government of Mid-Wake and that the surface had returned to some prehistoric Garden of Eden, a Paradise where opportunity was limitless. Tapes of the surface were openly available, showing what it was truly like, but the ones who insisted on a return to the surface insisted equally as militantly that the tapes were specifically shot in arctic and desert waste areas, that the vast majority of the Earth in what, before the conflict between the United States and the Soviet Union had begun five centuries ago, had been the Temperate Zones, was lush garden, fertile farmland.

Darkwood fought the feeling of nausea as calmly as he could.

He looked quickly toward the shoreline. The same white sand beach, the same palm trees, very much stunted, the same splotchy snow in the rocks. Overhead—he looked skyward—snow was still falling. It was an odd experience. As a snowflake touched his face, he drew back from it, then laughed at himself for reacting to something so normal—at least to some people.

What he could see of the lagoon itself and the island

98

seemed normal—not like before.

And for some reason that worried him all the more.

He took a last long breath to hold him while he adjusted his helmet, then resecured his helmet over his head to his suit, making the hermetic seal, a lightheadedness coming over him for an instant—predictable—as he switched to the suit's hemo sponge system. And he tucked beneath the surface, opening his wings and describing a cyclonic motion as he propelled himself downward toward where Sam Aldridge and the Marines were waiting on the bottom.

Darkwood moved into a huddle with them, within the circle they formed, their helmets touching so they could converse. To have used radio would have been to tempt fate. The helmets reliably picked up and transmitted the sympathetic vibrations of human speech, but there was always an eerie, hollow sound to the words, unnerving at times.

"What's the story, Captain?"

Darkwood turned his head slightly to glance toward Sam Aldridge. "Nothing out of the ordinary is visible on the beach or in the lagoon. Taking the working hypothesis a little further, they could either be waiting for us to break atmosphere or they might have other things on their minds entirely and not even know we're here. I'm betting on the latter. Which means we get ashore as quietly as we can, ditch our wings and the rest of our underwater gear, then head inland."

Darkwood could feel Aldridge's helmet nodding. Then Aldridge said, "All right—you heard the Captain, Marines. Any questions?"

There were none.

Aldridge nodded again. "Sergeant Richwood. Keep two men with you out here until you figure we're out of the water and deployed, then come in up the middle. Kowalski, Martinez, and O'Brien. Take the west end of

99

the lagoon. Hyde, Miller, and Luccesi—you guys got the east end. The rest of you come with me and the Captain. When we hit the beach, deploy first, then break atmosphere. Stick to those PV-26 shark guns our Soviet pals are so kind as to keep on giving us, the shark guns and knives unless push really comes to shove. I don't want any noise. Right? Let's swim out!"

And Sergeant Richwood—a big, blond-haired guy with oversized teeth that always made him look as though he were smiling—tapped two of the remaining Marines on the helmet, then moved off with them. The two penetration teams Sam Aldridge had designated started toward opposite ends of the lagoon. Darkwood tapped Aldridge on the helmet and Aldridge nodded. Darkwood let his wings fan out around him, beating them slowly, hovering for a moment. He adjusted his chest pack and the central section of his helmet shifted from normal vision to vision intensification, casting a surreal glow over everything on the bottom, the men as well.

Aldridge signaled his men into a standard assault V and Darkwood used wings, hands, and flippers to drop in beside Aldridge in the spot left for him, settling back to wing motion only to conserve strength as they moved ahead, the PV-26 strapped to his back. Aldridge's Marines towed buoyancy-compensated sleds, aboard the sleds Soviet AKM-96 rifles, a favorite for clandestine operations because the weapons were nearly as good as the American assault rifle and the ammunition could be scavenged in the field in operations against Soviet personnel. It was standard aboard Mid-Wake vessels that a substantial (not equal) number of AKM-96s and the American rifles were carried. Also aboard the floats were explosives and other gear that might be needed. Since there was no Army in any conventional five-centuries-ago sense, the

Marines with Navy assistance were it and had to be ready for whatever contingency arose. Darkwood had often thanked God that they habitually were.

He moved his wings in steady rhythm, the best way to make easy progress, working his chest pack controls periodically to make the shift from vision intensification to magnification when something curious on the bottom attracted his attention. There were fish here, not in abundance, certainly, but in significant variety. According to the latest scientific studies in ichthyology conducted with the help of the Navy, the marine population nearer to the surface was increasing rapidly, water quality steadily improving. If the Soviets launched one of their submarine-based nuclear missiles, all of that would likely end.

The bottom began shoaling rapidly, at times Darkwood helping himself along by actually touching the bottom and pushing himself ahead. The Marines towing the buoyancy-compensated sleds were having considerable difficulties moving them along and Darkwood and Aldridge fell back, physically assisting in propelling the sleds forward.

Jason Darkwood checked the luminous black face of the dual display Steinmetz on his wrist. It had cost him "big bucks" as Sam Aldridge had put it, but the watch was worth it. They had been in the swim for better than twenty minutes. They kept going, coral outcroppings rising like stalagmites in the photographs Darkwood had seen of terrestrial caves.

The shoaling became more dramatic, more pronounced, and Darkwood signaled Aldridge and his Marines to lay back while he swam ahead.

After another two hundred yards, Darkwood broke surface, not breaking atmosphere this time, instead actuating the defogging control for his helmet. Nothing on the beach. If all were normal, then where were the commando trainees? He had not just imagined the black-clad Soviet Spetznas troops.

Darkwood tucked under the surface, hovering for a moment, then swimming back toward Aldridge and the others. He signaled them ahead.

As they swam, Darkwood and Aldridge unlimbered their P-26 shark/antipersonnel guns.

The bottom rose rapidly, the current stronger above them, Darkwood moving on knees and elbows more than swimming, at last rising into a low crouch, breaking surface, Aldridge beside him. Darkwood hit his defogger, he and Aldridge and two other of the Marines covering the rest of the landing party who had to hand-carry the buoyancy-compensated sleds. And all of this was made the more difficult because there was no time to break atmosphere and the environment suit now worked to suffocate the wearer. Darkwood punched off vision intensification, realizing he was squinting with the added light on the surface.

Holding his breath, he ran now, a few paces behind Aldridge and the other Marines as they stormed up the beach, into a rocky niche twenty or twenty-five yards ashore.

Darkwood sank to his knees, breaking atmosphere instantly, the usual nauseated feeling momentarily displaced by the sheer necessity of gasping for breath.

He tore off his right glove. As he tried to breathe, he reached to the hermetically sealed container pouch on his environment suit. His right fist grasped the butt of the U.S. Government Model 2418 A2. He bit off his left glove and racked the slide, chambering the top 9mm Lancer Caseless off the fifteen round magazine. "So— lovely here, huh? Tropical island. A little falling snow." His breath steamed as he spoke. "And a temperature somewhere around freezing. Hey—my idea of a perfect vacation spot, right?" The other men were arming from the buoyancy comp sleds, assault rifles passed to them in a chain, the PV-26s still held because of the perceived need for silence.

Darkwood stripped away his environment suit, his black penetration suit worn beneath it. He shivered a little, grateful he'd brought the black synth-wool battle sweater with him. It was styled after the Wooly Pully sweaters popularized by the British Commandos during World War Two. And it was usually too warm to wear. He felt this time would be the exception. He took the hood from the compartment on his left thigh, pulled it on over his head, only the center portion of his face exposed. The spare magazines for the 9mm Lancer Caseless were still in his environment suit. He pulled them free, secured them to his chest pouches, replacing the fifteen-rounder with a thirty, putting the nearly full fifteen-rounder into the pouch at his thigh which formed the gun's holster. The handmade fighting knife he used was still sheathed to his environment suit. He resheathed it to the right calf of his penetration suit. He secured the grenade array to his left thigh, standard high explosive, smoke and sound/light.

He pulled the sweater on over his head. Fortunately, it was a V-neck to allow him access to the pouches on his chest pack and large enough. "You look like Lara Lynn," Aldridge quipped, cupping his hands in front of him as if they were supporting huge, pendulous breasts. Lara Lynn, aside from her other show-biz talents, was the hit of Mid-Wake entertainment for a less subtle reason, to which Aldridge referred.

"Thanks a bunch, Sam. Better than freezin' my ass off."

"I hear ya," Aldridge nodded.

Standard procedure for a penetration was that the suits, wings, helmets, and, if buoyancy comp sleds were used, those, too, were towed back to the relative safety of the water. Two of Aldridge's men were still in environment suits, helmets off, and as some of the other Marines began carrying the sleds back down the beach, security on either side of them, these two still in their environment suits rehelmeted, got a thumbs-up signal from Sam Aldridge, and ran after them.

Darkwood, Aldridge beside him, watched as the two men brought the sleds beneath the surface, then disappeared beneath the surface of the lagoon as well.

With the environment suits, of course, they could stay under water forever until they died of old age, boredom, or starvation. The suits were even designed so the wearer could urinate while wearing one, the urine storing in a pouch built into the leg of the suit. The starvation part was a potential problem, but the men could take turns breaking surface, then break atmosphere long enough to get down a nutrition pack.

Marines were taught to do that sort of thing, so Darkwood dismissed their problems. He had enough of his own.

"So, Jason—where's this training center supposed to be? They asked me to come here, never told me where it was."

"It should be well inland. That's all I know. The psych people figured that the best way to acclimate these guys to surface warfare was to get them as far away from the water as practical, so psychologically they would get used to a strictly terrestrial environment. So—we go inland and look for signs of the Marine Spetznas ahead of us."

"I'm sending one of the penetration teams around to the far side of the island to look for that Island Classer. If they don't see one, then what?"

"Hell if I know," Darkwood admitted as he shifted into his pack. "We improvise. Either that or I see an eye doctor when we get home." He had seen what he had seen. He knew that.

Darkwood took one of the AKM-96s and a bandolier of spare magazines, slinging the bandolier cross-body, right shoulder to left hip. He holstered the 2418 A2, secured it, then checked the action on the AKM-96. It was typical, sloppy but reliable. He rammed the magazine home.

Sam Aldridge was briefing one of the penetration teams for the tour around the island.

Darkwood stared ahead into the dense island growth. Palm trees, traditional jungle vegetation, pine trees, snow in the pine boughs. He judged the wind and temperature combined to be making a wind-chill factor about ten degrees or so below freezing. He pulled on his gloves.

"Ready," Aldridge said, suddenly beside him.

"Let's go," Darkwood nodded. They started out of the rocks, across the sand, into the odd-looking jungle. Men fanned out ahead of them, rifles slung, PV-26s in their hands for silent killing if needed.

If this were a full-scale Soviet invasion of the island, there was nothing to do but observe and get the hell out, Darkwood realized. But how had the Russians learned of Iwo Jima's secret? And how fast could a counterinvasion force be assembled. Aside from Sam Aldridge and a comparative handful of Marines, surface warfare experience was minimal. Had the Soviets been training for surface warfare at an accelerated pace?

He remembered some of the stories told by Doctor Rourke and Major Tiemerovna. Soviet armored vehicles and helicopter gunships. He shivered, and not from the cold, because the synth-wool sweater and the rapidity of his movement were doing their work.

Iwo Jima was a secret—but what if the secret it held were something no one at Mid-Wake had imagined.

105

Sam Aldridge, whose hobby had always been the western novels from the twentieth century, the movies of the period, all of that, stopped. "I think this is human urine, here."

There was an aggregate of bright green leaves with yellow fluid puddled in them. Maybe it was plant sap. Darkwood bent closer, smelled it. He looked at Aldridge. "If you tell me 'many horses pass here' or something—but you're right."

They weren't alone.

Chapter Sixteen

The specially modified German gunship's course followed north of and parallel to the Tropic of Cancer. Still there was no relief in the weather, snow falling, higher than normal winds (but not so high as to seriously hinder airigation) and lower than normal temperatures. An hour earlier, they landed on one of the smaller islands, snow accumulating on the tropical foliage. They used the landed time to check the gunship's systems, top off the synth-fuel and take a hasty meal of German freeze-dried rations, not as tasty as the Mountain House foods Rourke stocked at the Retreat, but just as nutritious. And again, they were airborne, Rourke giving Paul the stick as they flew on over the ocean.

Time dragged. Everywhere Rourke looked, everything seemed the same. If they were able to contact Mid-Wake, the American colony built as a scientific research station before The Night of The War, and Annie and Natalia and Otto Hammerschmidt had not been heard from—Rourke shivered. As any normal man, the initial impulse John Rourke had when he became a father was to think that a daughter was wonderful but a son was just a little bit more wonderful. And, as any normal man who was not bound by sexism or other forms of stupidity, he had realized a son and a daughter were equally wonderful. Annie was special to him beyond any words he could conjure. His daughter. And Natalia, whom he loved.

The monotony of gray sky and gray sea was suddenly broken.

There was an odd black shape on the horizon, not quite as large as one of the myriad islands which dotted the ocean surface below, more like a smallish atoll but something just not right about it.

"Paul. Take us a little north. Let's see what that is."

His movements deliberate, smoothly enough, Paul Rubenstein banked the helicopter off its course, toward the mysterious dark shape. They flew on for a few seconds. Rourke opened the cowling of his battered Zippo, rolled the striking wheel under his thumb, his eyes set on the gradually growing black shape. At last, he lit the tip of the thin dark tobacco cigar he'd had in his mouth for some time unlit, lit it in the blue-yellow flame, then flicked the cowling closed.

As he inhaled on the cigar, John Rourke's hands closed over the tubes of the German binoculars. He raised the binoculars and began to focus. The shape was definitely manmade because of the regularity of its— John Rourke lowered the binoculars. "Paul. That's a Soviet Island Class submarine." The machine jerked slightly and Rourke told his friend, "Take it easy. Hold your course. We wouldn't come in range of anything short of a missile for at least another minute." Rourke raised the binoculars again, the German gunship closing on the Soviet vessel.

Rourke let go of the binoculars, the binoculars hanging from the neck strap, his hands unrolling the chart by which they flew. The island off which the Soviet vessel lay was Iwo Jima . . .

*   *   *

A group of six men in the black uniforms of Marine Spetznas moved in single file along a rough trail cutting southward through the snow-splotched jungle, their AKM-96s slung to patroling carries. The trail wound along a sprawling ridgeline and, almost a half mile away from them, through his binoculars, Darkwood could see their faces clearly. They didn't look like Americans at all, whatever Americans looked like. Perhaps a mile farther back along the trail over which the six men moved, gray smoke rose skyward in a ragged column.

It was the smoke which first drew Darkwood, Aldridge, and the rest of Aldridge's Marine contingent into the island's more densely vegetated highlands.

The snow was deeper here, as well; and more snow was falling, larger flakes, bafflingly beautiful and diverse to Darkwood and the others who had never seen a snowfall in anything but an old film from five centuries ago, before their ancestors had come to man the scientific station of Mid-Wake and been stranded there by events beyond their control. A scientific research station between the islands of Midway and Wake, aimed at furthering man's knowledge of space-station construction and deep space travel, suddenly became the last actual outpost of the United States of America. A President, a bicameral legislature, a microcosm of the macrocosm. But it never snowed there.

As Jason Darkwood crouched behind a tall, wide-trunked, shallow-rooted tree he had no hope of identifying, he tasted another snowflake. There and gone. He looked at the tree, looked it up and down. There were many trees in Mid-Wake, all selected for their superior abilities to produce oxygen from carbon dioxide through photosynthesis beneath miniature artificial suns. Terrestrial botany was a specialty he had never studied. Few did. The broad, bright green leaves above him sagged beneath the weight of accumulated snow. Aldridge knelt beside him. "What do you think, Jason? Take 'em?" Aldridge's remark brought Darkwood's mind back to the situation at hand. And he momentarily regretted that because he wanted to remember the taste of snow, the feel of it.

"Yeah. But quietly if we can, Sam. We've got them outnumbered, but a firefight could turn that equation inside out real quick." Here in the highlands of the island, it actually was like some Paradise, like what the protestors insisted the entire surface of the Earth was within the Temperate Zones.

"I assume you want somebody to talk," Sam Aldridge continued.

"Yeah, that'd be nice, Sam—and I don't feel like having them activate those self-destruct charges they carry on their bodies and taking us with them. Rifle butts and fists, knives if you have to. And don't forget about me."

Sam Aldridge grinned at him and nodded . . .

With Aldridge and four other Marines, the rest of the force waiting a hundred yards farther up the trail, Jason Darkwood slipped into the foliage overlooking the trail from the highground, waiting. There was a joke that had been going around ever since it was first discovered five centuries ago that the Soviet Union had a base beneath the Pacific Ocean as well, a base considerably larger, more technologically advanced (at the time), and better populated: One American can lick any dozen of the Commies. Darkwood imagined the joke was really older than five centuries, but surprisingly the joke became an operational principle. With more men at his disposal, why had Sam Aldridge only asked for four volunteers (everyone volunteered and

110

Aldridge took his pick) and left the remainder of the men under his Sergeant. Still more bizarre, Darkwood had said nothing, simply gone along as one of the six. Six Americans, five of them Marines, versus six Soviet Marine Special Forces personnel was taking unfair advantage—if you believed in the joke.

Three of the Marines moved up a dozen yards or so along the trail, Aldridge and Lance Corporal Lannigan staying in position beside Darkwood, flanking him. The palms of Darkwood's hands sweated inside his gloves as he grasped the AKM-96 more tightly.

Six against six, or seventy-two lying in ambush for six—if you believed the joke.

He peered between two snow-laden leaves, the sounds of snow crunching under the booted feet of the Marine Spetznas detail. He'd read in books about the sounds of snow crunching under boots, not noticed the sound beneath his own boots or those of Aldridge's Marines, noticed the sounds now. He could see the face of the lead man, not necessarily the leader because of his position in the file, but obviously the leader because of his rank. He was a Sergeant.

The remaining five men were younger, not as experienced-looking, not as tough-looking either. Sam Aldridge tapped Darkwood on the shoulder, pointed toward the Sergeant, then tapped himself on the chest and nodded. Darkwood shrugged his shoulders and eyebrows. If Sam Aldridge felt he had to brace the toughest-looking one of the six, good for him.

Coming.

They didn't seem to like each other, either that or they were tremendously disciplined, each man's face set in a neutral expression, no idle chatter, no laughter.

Jason Darkwood looked at Sam Aldridge, figuring Aldridge would take the lead, make the first move since his chosen target was the man to get. Aldridge flexed his fists over his rifle and sprang up from his crouch, hurtling himself through the foliage and down into the trail in a cloud of suddenly displaced snow, moving as if his legs were made of coiled springs, landing on his feet in the center of the trail less than a yard from the Soviet Sergeant.

The Sergeant froze. Aldridge snapped the butt of his AKM-96 across the jaw of the Russian and the Russian fell back. "Now!" Aldridge shouted. Darkwood jumped through the foliage, not nearly as gracefully, he realized, his body impacting the body of one of the Marine Spetznas as the man turned toward him, Darkwood sprawling across him as they fell across the trail, the Russian behind Darkwood's man tripping, falling over them as Darkwood rolled away, hammering a right cross into his target's jaw.

Lance Corporal Lannigan was locked in combat with the man who had tripped over Darkwood and the Russian. As Darkwood reached for his man, he saw something he realized he'd never forget for the rest of his life—however long or short that might be. The Marine Spetznas Sergeant hadn't fallen down, simply stood there, Sam Aldridge in freeze frame with his body poised for a forward butt stroke. The Marine Spetznas Sergeant threw down his rifle and drew his Marine Spetznas-issue fighting knife, in Russian saying something Darkwood translated as roughly equivalent to "Eat Shit, American black bastard cocksucker!"

Darkwood couldn't take his eyes from Sam Aldridge and the Russian. Aldridge threw down his rifle, drew his knife. Sam Aldridge was descended from one of the first Marines at Mid-Wake, the man a Marine officer and deep diving specialist. Sam Aldridge's knife was a copy of that five-centuries-old Ka-Bar U.S.M.C. fighting knife Aldridge's ancestor had brought to Mid-

Wake as a personal weapon when the colony had begun, identical to the one taken from Aldridge when he was captured by the Soviets. The knife was fabulously expensive, Parkerizing (phosphate coating) almost a lost art, the leather for the washered handle rare. Aldridge snarled—in Russian—"Your mother, man!"

Darkwood saw his man moving at the far right edge of his peripheral vision and he rolled away, the Marine Spetznas throwing himself at Darkwood, his issue knife in his fist. For the first time, Darkwood realized he'd lost hold of his rifle. He was Navy, not a Marine. In the Marines they taught you to hold on to your rifle like a lonely man might hold on to his organ on a long night. In the Navy, a rifle was something you learned to shoot, then said, "That's nice" about and forgot.

The Marine Spetznas lunged. Darkwood came to his feet, a handful of trail gravel, rotted leaves, and snow in his left fist. He hurtled the mixture toward his opponent's face. As the man recoiled, Darkwood's hand moved his knife from its sheath. Many of the custom knives made at Mid-Wake and all of the production knives from Mid-Wake's one knife factory were like Sam Aldridge's knife, copies of knives from the past. Darkwood's knife was at once totally different, yet no exception. When Nathaniel Darkwood had come to Mid-Wake, he'd brought with him the experiences from a lifetime of adventure, and this lifetime's trophies. Nathaniel Darkwood's weapons collection and other collections resided in the New Smithsonian. Jason Darkwood, heir to the Darkwood "estate," still owned that collection, borrowed the knife which Darkwood had truly used from among the dozens which Darkwood had possessed, had that knife copied by Mid-Wake's finest custom knifesmith. As the Marine Spetznas lunged, Jason Darkwood stepped back, pivoted, caught the man's knife against his.

The Marine Spetznas fell back.

Jason Darkwood's eyes focused on the Russian's eyes. The Russian's eyes flickered and Darkwood lunged, the blade in Jason Darkwood's hand an identical duplicate of his ancestor's Randall Smithsonian Bowie. The tip of Darkwood's blade crossed the inside right forearm of the Marine Spetznas and the knife fell from the Russian's suddenly limpened fingers, a scream of pain issuing from his mouth, wide open in shock. Darkwood stepped inside the Russian's suddenly vanished guard, with the butt of his knife impacting the base of the Russian's jaw. Darkwood's left knee smashed upward. As the Russian's head snapped back, the Russian's body jackknifed forward. With a chop from the Bowie's primary edge or even the blunt impact from the butt of his knife across the back of the Marine Spetznas' neck, the man would have died. Instead, Jason Darkwood let him fall.

Mechanically, Darkwood looked around him, the other Marine Spetznas personnel subdued, all except for the Sergeant who fought Sam Aldridge. And Darkwood's eyes riveted to them. They moved in a classic knife fighter's circle, testing each other's reaction times with feigned lunges, withdrawals. The Soviet Sergeant held his blade easily, as though he weren't really holding it at all, as though it were simply part of his hand.

Darkwood wiped his own blade clean across the back of his enemy's uniform, sheathed it quickly as he reached for his AKM-96. Darkwood rose to his full height as he brought the AKM-96 up, holding the rifle by the barrel near the front sight. Darkwood swung, the butt of the assault rifle impacting the Soviet Sergeant across the shoulder blades in midswing, Darkwood following through, a groan of pain from the

114

Soviet Sergeant as his body crumpled, then spilled forward into the virgin snow by the side of the trail. As the man rolled onto his back, his face contorted into a mask of pain, Darkwood had the rifle inverted, the muzzle almost touching the tip of the man's nose. In Russian, Darkwood told him, "You guessed correctly, Comrade. There is no wish to make noise with a gun. In your case, there can be an exception. Try me."

The Marine Spetznas Sergeant raised his hands, his knife falling from his fingers into the snow.

Chapter Seventeen

Damien Rausch's right first finger touched the rear trigger of the Steyr-Mannlicher SSG. The 7.62mm sniper rifle was one of only two in the strategic supply cache, the location of which he and his men had discovered through the cooperation of Commander Christopher Dodd. The M-16 rifles, although, like the sniper rifle, five centuries old, had decidedly greater potential for his overall purpose. But sniper rifles could be useful. Now, for example, he thought. His finger snapped off the rear trigger, then eased forward along the edge of the guard, just beside the front trigger, now set to go with the very slightest pressure.

The German vision intensification scope, conveniently enough mounted to the Austrian-origin rifle with only a slight machining modification to the rails on the receiver, showed Dodd's yellow nemesis clearly enough—this Akiro Kurinami. Kurinami was only a Lieutenant, a very young man, yet Dodd perceived Kurinami as his arch rival for control of the Eden Project. Once there was an appropriate lull in the battle between the Soviets and their growing list of allied enemies, Dodd was convinced free elections for the leadership of Eden Base would be demanded. And

Kurinami, as Dodd told it, would run against him, would win. But, if Kurinami were out of the picture, there would be no clear rival to Dodd's leadership. If elections did come, Dodd envisioned himself the easy victor in the absence of the Japanese Naval Lieutenant.

Kurinami moved along a steeply rising road, toward the face of a mountain. Was this actually the entrance to the survival retreat of the infamous Doctor John Rourke?

Rausch wondered.

And what things of interest might this place contain?

All things might be of value in the struggle to restore to power in New Germany those who followed the philosophy of The Leader, specifically himself. If he shot Kurinami, who according to Dodd knew the secret entrance to Rourke's mountain retreat, the secret would die with Kurinami.

Rausch wondered.

He released the SSG's five-round magazine, only four rounds remaining in the rotary feeding box. He worked the bolt, ejecting the chambered round, catching it in midflight.

He closed the bolt and snapped off the front trigger with the chamber empty.

Damien Rausch rolled onto his back in the snow. Beside him, one of his men began, "But, Herr Rausch—"

Rausch only smiled as he remagazined the loose round. "Watch him." He put the magazine back in place, then gave it a firm slap . . .

Akiro Kurinami's bones ached him, as did every muscle that wasn't numbed from the cold. He kept walking, Elaine's face in his thoughts, her face and the knowledge that the Retreat's main entrance was just a little farther away all that kept him going, had kept him going as he walked on and on. The snow fell more heavily and there was little Soviet helicopter traffic, especially since nightfall. If somehow he were attacked, he wouldn't be able to activate the controls of the pistol at his side.

He kept walking, not thinking about moving his feet, not thinking about anything except the woman he loved and the warmth and food of the Retreat. But first the radio, of course, to contact the German command outside Eden Base, warn them that an unprecedented number of Soviet gunships was gathering for an all-out attack on Eden Base and their own airfield.

Perhaps Colonel Mann could be contacted, divert some of the forces of New Germany in time to do something.

That was the only hope.

He ran the procedure through his mind for opening the entrance to the Retreat, almost fearful to do so because, he realized, if he made the picture too real in his mind perhaps his mind would withdraw to that and he would lie down in the snow and die while fantasizing he was opening the entrance door.

But he would have little time to open the door when he finally reached the Retreat, little time because all of his will and momentum would be drained.

The rock. He would have to move the rock. Two rocks. Like some ancient Egyptian tomb or something. The large boulder that could be pushed away easily enough by a strong man. Then the squared-off rock. Pushing against that was considerably more difficult. There would be a rumbling that seemed to come from deep within the mountain itself, and the granite on which he stood would begin to lower, and as it did, a slab of rock within the side of the mountain would move away, inward.

And then rest.

Akiro Kurinami kept walking . . .

Damien Rausch and three of his men moved along the trail on foot, keeping just far enough behind Kurinami that if the Japanese naval aviator were to begin to turn around, they could duck out of sight.

"The injection kit is ready?"

"Yes, Herr Rausch," the man beside him panted, breathless-sounding from the exertion.

"He is not to be killed."

"Yes, Herr Rausch."

Damien Rausch felt a thrill he rarely experienced. As a youth, he had studied archaeology with a passion, that passion only secondary to his passion for the Fatherland, his devotion to The Leader.

Five centuries ago, a man who still lived, the man chiefly responsible for the deposing of The Leader with the aid of the traitorous Wolfgang Mann and his officers, had built this place to weather the inevitable coming storm. And, inside it, he and his family and a Jew and a Communist had survived, slept much like the Eden Project personnel had slept in their criogenic chambers aboard the space shuttles.

What mysteries did this place hold? Greater things than he could obtain from the Eden Project stores, greater wisdom than he could avail himself of from the Eden Project computers. Here was not an outline of the past; here was the past, perfectly preserved just as it had been when it was placed here.

Once Kurinami stopped and began to open the secret entrance, they would strike. And the thoughts of what lay beyond that entrance tantalized him.

Chapter Eighteen

Paul Rubenstein sat at the controls of the German helicopter gunship. Snow fell heavily. At the south center of the island of Iwo Jima, there was smoke, a lot of it, rising skyward in a heavy column, so heavy that the column reached considerable height before fully dissipating on the strong crosswinds. They finished the circle of the island, John Rourke aware of the fact that his friend was having trouble keeping the machine under control, ready to seize control if needed, but letting Paul get the experience. They flew only close enough that Rourke could get some perception of detail through the powerful German binoculars, but hopefully not close enough to draw attention to themselves from the ground.

"What the heck's goin' on? Why the smoke?" Paul Rubenstein ruminated.

John Rourke couldn't resist it. "Well, where there's smoke, as they say. No. Good question, Paul. If it were only that Island Class Soviet submarine, I'd say they were stopping for some more or less mundane purpose. But the smoke in the middle of the island makes it look like something else. I'll take the controls—we're going in. I'm banking on their sensing equipment all being sea-oriented. If that is the case, the higher altitude we come in at, the less chance we'll be spotted. Then we

121

drop altitude over the center of the island."

"You've got the stick," Paul told him, Rourke taking control. "I'll get our gear ready."

John Rourke only nodded. Time could not be wasted, but if the Island Classer were in combat, their only possible opponents would be from Mid-Wake. And that meant a chance to contact Mid-Wake, more rapidly, more surely. If not— And his eyes squinted toward the hulking black shape of the submarine.

Rourke started the German gunship climbing. He could run with silenced rotors once they were over the island in the event the Island Classer had put a party ashore. If the Island Classer hadn't, what was the origin of the smoke? He glanced aft. Paul Rubenstein was checking the M-16s.

The actual insertion of the needle was done by Lance Corporal Lannigan, Aldridge ordering him to. Jason Darkwood was relieved that no one had expected him to do it. Few things made him feel squeamish, but watching a hypodermic injection was unfortunately one of them. Since the Marine Spetznas Sergeant was the ranking man, he was the logical place to start. As with many truth drugs, it was necessary to supplement the dosage of the drug as the interrogation progressed, all of this rather subjective. Lannigan was the logical man for the detail since he was studying pharmacology and planned to pursue a career in pharmacy after his stint in the Corps. The drug used for special operations such as this where an enemy was interrogated in the field was identical to the most popular of the Soviet truth serums, Mid-Wake official reasoning here quite sound, Darkwood had always thought. It was possible that any truth serum Mid-Wake medical scientists might independently devise could be compromised. Then it would be a simple matter for Soviet personnel habitually given access to sensitive information to be conditioned against the effects of such a drug. But the Russians would never condition their own people against their own truth drug. Such just didn't happen in a police state. And, so far, the Soviets hadn't gotten wise to the fact that the Americans at Mid-Wake were using that drug's identical duplicate.

Lannigan removed the needle from the intravenous receptacle he had installed. But Jason Darkwood turned around too soon, seeing it, and his stomach started to go. Darkwood looked skyward to take his eyes away from the scene. And he caught a glimpse of a dark shape against the gray clouds just passing out of sight over the trees. "Either the Russians have secretly been growing gigantic birds, or this is the last refuge of the prehistoric pterodactyl or one of those helicopter things just passed over our heads."

"Right," Sam Aldridge laughed. "We would have heard it. Remember those ones before? We heard those. Naw— And anyway, only the surface-based Russians—aww shit."

"My sentiments exactly," Darkwood nodded to his friend.

"The Spetznas Sergeant should be ready to talk in—" The young Marine consulted his watch. "Just about another ten or fifteen seconds, sir," Lannigan said.

Darkwood looked back. Maybe the Marine Spetznas Sergeant would have some exceedingly interesting things to say . . .

There was a ridge leading from the island highlands and, near to the height of the ridge, the gray smoke still rose. The search for a suitable landing area had taken considerably longer than Rourke had wanted, but the wind was increasing, making precise maneuvering more difficult and visibility was dropping, the storm

123

intensifying. At last an opening in the snow-splotched tree canopy presented itself and Rourke brought the gunship in, less than a mile from the mysterious smoke, landing in a shoaled area through which a wide, shallow stream ran. Not the best landing site, but adequate. Snow stuck to the ground in many areas and the broad bright-green-leafed tropical foliage weighed heavily downward under its weight, the high winds above the forest canopy fell as occasional strong gusts on the ground.

"You stick with the machine," John Rourke told Paul Rubenstein, Rourke beginning to slip into his coat beside the opened fuselage door.

"Wait a minute," the younger man said. "Fine. You taught me how to keep the helicopter on course in level flight. I don't know how to get one of these off the ground with any degree of reliability, let alone land it. Remember the last time I took a helicopter up?";

Paul had done a ridiculously brave thing, taking a gunship airborne to provide cover against Soviet helicopters as they attacked the returning Eden Project shuttles. And, as a result, Paul nearly died. John Rourke felt a smile cross his lips, despite almost losing his best friend. Sometimes Rourke thought his muscles still ached from getting Paul out of the burning helicopter. "You suggest, then?"

"Either we both go and set the remote defenses to keep tabs on the chopper or just I go by myself."

Rourke considered Paul's words for a moment. Then, almost thinking out loud, said, "Yes, but if we set the remote defenses, and someone actually does arrive to tamper with the chopper, the wrong kind of tampering could cause the machine to explode and we could be stranded here with no way to continue the search for Annie and Natalia and Otto. Logic dictates you go alone." Rourke shrugged out of his parka, helping Paul Rubenstein to start gearing up.

Chapter Nineteen

Natalia Anastasia Tiemerovna moved restlessly in her drug-induced sleep. Annie Rourke Rubenstein watched her. There was nothing else to do, all the medical supplies that might be needed if there were enemy action about the Mid-Wake submarine checked, ready, the *Reagan* "steaming" toward Mid-Wake. She considered that. "Steaming" was probably still correct, because presumably the nuclear power was used to generate steam, the steam then turning the screws which propelled the vessel along beneath the waves.

She felt better in the borrowed skirt and shirt, Doctor Margaret Barrow close enough to her in body configuration that the fit was good. But skirts were so short here, the uniform skirt ending just below the knee.

She studied her legs beneath the hem of her skirt. She guessed they were pretty. Paul had told her they were. And, as she had moved through the submarine earlier, when Commander Sebastian, the First Officer, had taken her for a cup of coffee, explained what was going on, she had noticed some of the men of the ship's company looking at her.

Her hair was considerably longer than that of any of the women aboard the *Reagan,* the women of the bridge crew "in regs" as Margaret Barrow put it. But even Margaret Barrow's hair, longer than that of the other women, was comparatively short. She wondered if that were the style all over Mid-Wake or just in the military. She had gone to Mid-Wake very briefly, aboard a submarine just like this. After her father had returned there, he announced that he had been diagnosed as having radiation-induced thyroid cancer (her heart had gone to her mouth), but that the medical arts at Mid-Wake had progressed to the point where such cancers were wholly curable and easily so. With her mother, her father, and Paul accompanying, she had traveled to Mid-Wake, staring through the video projection as though it were a window to the sea because it looked just like that. Paul, and Michael and Natalia, too, of course, had all been checked earlier, given a clean bill of health. Her own examination— barely noticeable as an examination at all—had shown her in perfect health, as were her mother and the baby. As a result of the examination, it was learned coincidentally that the child her mother carried would be a boy.

Her father still referred to the child sexlessly— neither he nor her mother had ever believed in finding out before delivery, an option available more or less even when she—Annie—and her brother Michael were still to be born.

Her eyes had returned to Natalia and still watched her. She was very beautiful, even ill as she was. Annie had brushed out Natalia's hair, arranged it as Natalia usually did herself. The lids of Natalia's eyes fluttered and there was a momentary glimpse of her dark, pansy-blue eyes. The pupils were dilated.

"What's the matter?"

Annie looked up, momentarily startled. It was Doctor Barrow. "Nothing, Maggie. I just didn't hear you come in."

"Worried about your friend?" Maggie Barrow smiled, digging her hands into the side pockets of her lab coat, leaning back, then sitting on the edge of a hospital gurney, crossing her legs, her skirt shooting up half the length of her thighs. "I wish I could say there was something more we could do to help Major Tiemerovna, but I can't think of anything that can be done here."

"She's had such a sad life."

Maggie Barrow nodded, sympathetically. "I understood from a brief conversation with your father once that you're a sensitive."

At Mid-Wake, after the physical examination, they had asked her to indulge in what amounted to game playing with a computer monitor, a half dozen people she was barely introduced to trotted past her. "I'm not a mind reader. No. It's just that with people I know, I care about—and for some reason very strongly with Natalia—I can sometimes see what they see, feel what they feel, sense danger. Or sometimes I'll dream, and in the dream I'll see what's happening. I think as it's happening. There's never been any desire to check it out anymore, even if there'd been the time."

"You see things happening in dreams?"

"Uh-huh. But only if it's something that involves very strong emotions. I can't read cards— Well, I can, but only with people I know."

"What do you mean?" Maggie Barrow asked.

Annie stood up, smoothed her skirt along her thighs. "I mean, I can't sit down with somebody I don't know and have them turn cards over and not show them to me but just read what they are through them seeing the cards. But, I could do that with somebody I'm close to.

127

Like sometimes it's terrible, you know?"

"Why?"

Annie smiled. "Paul—my husband. I have to force myself not to read his thoughts, sometimes. I mean, sometimes I'll just be sitting there and he's near me and I'm not really thinking about anything and then suddenly I know what he's thinking and I force myself not to because it's like looking in somebody's bedroom or something."

"And you can do this with Major Tiemerovna?"

"It's like we can communicate without talking. It's different with her. There was this man—he was a traitor. He was part of the Eden Project but he was a traitor. And he kidnapped me. And I escaped from him—I, ahh—I killed him. But I learned how I should do it from going into Natalia's mind with my mind. It scared the crap out of me," Annie Rubenstein laughed. "But he scared me more. So, I did it. I went in—I really—ahh—"

"How do you mean 'went in'?"

"Just what I said. I talked to Natalia about it afterward. And, for some reason she didn't understand at the time, she just started thinking about this time she had been captured by these revolutionaries or something and they were going to kill her but first one of them was going to rape her. Well, I learned from her experience. He was—ahh—and when he tried, this man Blackburn," and Annie shuddered thinking of it. "I stabbed him. Just like Natalia did."

Margaret Barrow's hands clutched at the hem of her skirt as she uncrossed her legs, pulling it down nearer to her knees, her shoulders hunching. "That's scary."

"Yeah. I know." There was something in Maggie's eyes, beyond being scared, Annie Rubenstein thought. But it was only that, a thought.

"Are you afraid? I mean, afraid of what you can do?"

"Sometimes. I'm just afraid I'll get better at it. And that scares me to death," Annie told her honestly.

"What's Major Tiemerovna thinking now?"

Annie licked her lips, swallowed. "Ahh—" She turned around, feet and legs together, feeling suddenly very cold. And she looked at Natalia. "I don't know if I should—ahh—"

"Trust me," Maggie Barrow prodded. "I've got an idea. But try this, okay?"

Annie licked her lips again and nodded. She closed her eyes. She thought about Natalia, picturing Natalia in her mind, picturing what Natalia could be thinking about. Inside herself, Annie saw her father's face. It kept appearing and disappearing, appearing and disappearing, in one place, then another place, out of darkness and out of fire. He was wearing his sunglasses, the dark-lenses aviator-style glasses he wore so frequently because he was very light-sensitive. She saw his face more clearly now, and reflected in the glasses—"No—no!"

Annie Rubenstein fell to her knees, the floor cold feeling through her stockings, her arms hugged tight to her chest. And she felt Maggie Barrow's hands on her shoulders, felt her kneeling beside her. "Annie?"

"I saw—saw inside—inside Natalia's dreams."

"Was it—I mean—"

"In my father's glasses. I saw—" Everything was moving around her and she felt cold and hot all at the same time and when she opened her eyes everything looked green for an instant and then—

129

Chapter Twenty

Paul Rubenstein dropped to a crouch along the side of the naturally formed trail on the ridgeline. A few hundred yards back, he had discovered footprints and other markings in the snow and on the brush, that a group of men in military gear had passed this way. They seemed not very good at concealing their passage, nor the best woodsmen, either. He backtracked them for a hundred yards or so toward the higher ground above the ridgeline. At times, it seemed evident that when two paths of travel presented themselves, both on surface analysis seeming equal but one the clear choice of the experienced outdoorsman, more often than not the poorer choice was chosen. Paul Rubenstein recognized the look, remembering how comparatively short a time ago—despite the fact that an objective five centuries had passed—he had been grossly inexperienced. He had learned quickly because he had the best teacher and because it was either learn or die. These men whose trail he now paralleled would learn quickly, too—or die.

Signs of a scuffle in the snow. With the point of the Gerber MK II he habitually carried he cleared away freshly fallen snow very gently, finding some traces of blood. Beside the trail, someone had either sat or fallen. In other places, too many footprints, only partially drifted over, obscured body prints.

A fight involving a dozen men or more. After that, the footprints that he had followed intersected here, either joining or following the participants. These footprints in some cases overlayed the earlier prints. Two different patterns in the boots, only two, clearly indicating two military groups. He could kick himself for not memorizing the sole patterns of the Mid-Wake combat boots.

He looked to right and left, up and down the trail and in the rocks above. Clearly, one type of the footprints had come from the region where the gray smoke—still rising near the horizon—originated. And now those footprints along with many others, the second tread pattern in substantially greater numbers than the first, moved toward the smoke again.

Paul Rubenstein slung his M-16 behind him, loosening the sling of the Schmeisser submachine gun. At close quarters, it was the better choice. And it would be close quarters crossing through the forest—it was impossible to think of it as jungle with the snow. But crossing through rather than taking the ridgeline trail might get him to the source of the smoke ahead of the force taking the trail.

He left the trail, careful to blend his own footprints in as best as possible with the mélange of footprints already there, doubling back, leaving the trail at the first opportunity where his doing so wouldn't be immediately and obviously noticeable. If John Rourke decided to follow him, that was a different story. Where the terrain allowed, he kept to a jog trot, time slipping away . . .

*   *   *

John Rourke, an M-16 chamber loaded on either side of him, sat cross-legged on the cabin floor of the German gunship. He was stripping and cleaning his pistols, one at a time. Both of the Detonics mini-guns were already finished and he started the first of the two full-sized Detonics Scoremasters. He removed the magazine, worked the slide to verify visually and tactilely that there was an empty chamber, then drew the slide rearward until the slidestop and disassembly both lined up, then pushed out the slide stop. He took the slide forward on its rails, removing it from the frame, then set to separating recoil springs and guide rod from the barrel, then removing the barrel from the slide. With his German-duplicated Break-Free CLP, he began swabbing out the bore. A detailed stripping was not necessary.

The Island Class Soviet submarine. Why was it here, he wondered? The smoke was the key. Perhaps the Soviets had merely surfaced as they might routinely do and some sharp-eyed person on the sail had noticed the smoke coming from the center of the island. Perhaps only a lightning strike. But John Rourke doubted that.

He suspected a scenario that might fit: either Mid-Wake or their Soviet antagonists had established some sort of base on Iwo Jima and the two forces were in conflict, perhaps accidental. If some full-scale operation were in progress, why was the Soviet submarine surfaced? And, to the best he could determine with equipment aboard the gunship, why was there only one? There was no sign of the smaller submarines of Mid-Wake at all in evidence.

He wiped off the parts, then began reassembly. In the days of normalcy (what little of that there had been), one of his favorite things to do in an off moment (what little of those there had been) was to read the latest gun magazine.

One of his favorite writers, Jan Libourel, had always struck him as an erudite man. Perhaps, Rourke reflected, that was because his own opinions often coincided with Libourel's. As Rourke reloaded the Scoremaster, then began to safe and disassemble the second one of the two full sized .45s, he realized oddly that he missed the days of normalcy very much. *Petersen's Handguns,* which Libourel edited, could never be delivered to his door by the postman—he had no door except the rock slab which masked the entrance to the Retreat. And, there were no more postmen.

Chapter Twenty-One

It was necessary to seek the higher ground, and not much ground was higher here except those places where a mountain goat might well have moved comfortably, but no other creature. Damien Rausch, two of his men flanking him, clambered along a narrow ledge, moving slowly upward, Kurinami lost from sight here. Rausch's field glasses—fortunately still cased—slammed against the rock wall. He kept climbing.

At last, the ledge narrowed, leveled slightly, a sick feeling in the pit of Rausch's stomach beginning to dissipate slightly. The snow made the footing treacherous and if he had fallen from the ledge— He would have to make his way down, but he dismissed thoughts of the descent until the descent would be upon him.

There was a tongue-shaped outcropping. It would overlook where Kurinami had stopped, where somehow the entrance to Rourke's mountain survival retreat had to be.

Rausch moved out along the outcropping, at first in a crouch then to his knees and elbows, crawling the last few yards through the cold wetness of the snow. A vicious wind howled, ghostly sounding through niches in the rock below and above and all around him.

Rausch uncased his binoculars, began to adjust the focus as he settled them on the Japanese Naval Aviator.

The Japanese was rolling away some large boulder. Beside Rausch, one of his men whispered, "Should we—"

"No—wait." Rausch lowered his field glasses for an instant, blew the snow from the objective lenses, raised them. Now Kurinami had moved left, was bracing his body against a flat stone, pushing against it. The man looked incredibly tired, bone-weary. Rausch bet with himself and won. Kurinami collapsed to his knees beside the rock. But still, the Japanese threw his weight against it, standing as the rock began slightly to budge.

And as the rock moved, the ground beneath the Japanese's feet began to sink. Rausch blinked. A segment of the mountain wall behind Akiro Kurinami began to move inward. The Herr Doctor's lair.

Kurinami stumbled toward the opening, disappeared through it. Rausch used his radio. "Close in! Close in now! Quickly!"

A red light filtered through the snow, washing the ground before the opening in the mountain wall.

Rausch's stomach knotted again as he pushed himself to his feet, ran in a low crouch and then came to his full height, leaving the outcropping, the men who had accompanied him barely keeping up with him.

Rausch reached the rock ledge, took each step with care and with all the haste caution would allow, reached the narrower portion of the edge. The footing was impossibly slick and the snow-slicked rock wall provided little handhold for him. He moved downward along the ledge nevertheless skidding, slipping, catching his balance, freezing in place for an instant of fear, then forcing his legs to move again.

He reached the base of the ledge, jumped, came

down in a crouch in deep snow, spit snow from his lips, ran around the side of the rock wall.

There it was, the opening, red light still flooding the snow-packed ground, the depression still in the ground where a portion of it had lowered when the Japanese pushed the squarish rock.

"We have him, Herr Rausch! We have the Japanese officer, Herr Rausch!" The shout came from inside where the red light originated.

Rausch slipped once, caught himself, ran, reached the opening, stepped through.

An enormous set of double doors. They were made of steel or some other type of metal, looking to be electroplated as well. They were massive. Some type of sensors; he was uncertain of their purpose. They were mounted into the living rock. There was a video camera. Its housing appeared antique.

There were combination dials on the doors. He had seen photographs of such devices. They were not electronic, had to be worked precisely to open unless the doors which they sealed shut were blown down.

The Japanese lay in a heap before the doors, unconscious or dead. The doors were closed.

Rausch's fists balled closed, then open, then closed again. His stomach still churned from the descent. He was slightly affected by heights, always had been, usually conquered the fear more easily. He walked toward the man he'd left in charge, stared into his gray eyes for a long moment, then backhanded him across the mouth with his open hand, driving the man to his knees. "Idiot!"

And Rausch turned to stare at the doors.

Chapter Twenty-Two

Michael Rourke stood in the open entrance for the airlock of the hermetically sealed tent, Maria Leuden shivering beside him. A J7-V was going airborne.

Impulsively, Michael Rourke waved after it, wondering if he would see his mother ever again, ever know the child she carried in her womb who would be his sibling.

"Michael?"

"You're cold. I'll take you inside."

"I love you, Michael."

Michael Rourke turned toward her, his arms enfolding her. She raised her head, her lips slightly parted. He bent his face over hers, looking into her eyes for a moment. They were beautiful eyes. "I love you, Michael."

His mouth touched gently at hers, then harder, his arms crushing her against him, his lips touching her throat, her hair, her coat opening. He opened his. She pressed her body against him and he closed his coat around them.

He held her, his eyes moving toward the night sky, the J7-V's running lights all but lost in the swirling snow surrounding the tent, filling the night.

In moments, with Rolvaag and a small team of German commandos and a unit of volunteers who survived the Soviet assault on Hekla Base, he would go into the night. Rolvaag, as best they could understand him, told of something that might have been tunnels, lava flows which led beneath the cone.

Michael Rourke kissed Maria Leuden hard on the mouth.

Her lips touched at his cheek. He could barely hear her as she whispered, "I love you, Michael Rourke."

"I love you, Fraulein Doctor Leuden," and he held her very tightly. Someone would come, tell him it was time to move out. He would wait until then, holding her.

Chapter Twenty-Three

Paul Rubenstein realized that he was tiring less than normally he would have. In the tropics, the air was normally more dense, more oxygen rich, and, despite the generally thinned atmosphere, the correlation held true. Physical activity was easier.

He reached a rise above the ridge, below him seeing the trailing edge of a column of men, the column disappearing behind a wall of trees.

Another column was clearly visible, the column of smoke. He would reach it before these men, whoever they were, reached it. He uncased the German binoculars, was still unable to see what lay at the base of the column of smoke, what its origin might be, because it originated above his current position.

Paul Rubenstein cased the binoculars and ran on. What a peaceful scene, he thought—a jungle filling up with snow, snow which might be radioactive. John had used the gunship's sensors to make atmospheric samplings and they had shown negative results, but there was always a chance that the snow in some new cloud might contain radioactive dust particles. And why was it snowing where normally—what was normal? he didn't really remember—where normally the weather was eternal summer.

"Skiing on the beach at Waikiki," Paul Rubenstein said to himself aloud, quickening his pace . . .

The sensors monitoring the network of automatic electronic systems, which both kept track of the mechanical condition of the gunship and protected it from tampering with everything from electrical charges through the gunship's skin to an explosive device equivalent in impact to several sticks of dynamite, also served as a perimeter alarm.

The German gunship's perimeter alarm system was activated now.

John Rourke put down the gunship's shop manual; it made for difficult reading in technical German, but with the aid of a solid dictionary and the video display supplement which overlayed one system into another and put the systems into motion where appropriate, it was intelligible.

He stood up, hitting the control panel switch to begin warming the synth-oil in the crankcase, then peered through the Plexiglas where the snow covering allowed. The interior surface of the glasslike substance was designed to resist fogging. It seemed to do that well. He supposed someone not born in the twentieth century would simply have activated the video displays fed from the cameras mounted beneath the main rotor, rather than just try to look out something as ordinary as a window. But old habits died hard.

He saw nothing.

This didn't console him.

One of the Scoremasters in his right fist, he sat at the consoles and began activating the gunship's systems for take-off. Before the Night of the War, a constant source of amusement for him had been movies in which

the hero or bad guy ran up to an aircraft sitting un-
attended on some lonely runway, jumped behind the
controls, switched on the engines and took off, just as
someone might have done with an automobile.

He checked the video monitoring system. There was
movement farther downstream, shifting patches of
black amid the green of the leaves and the white of the
snow. "Hmm."

He began checking systems, his eyes alternating
from the control panels to the video monitors. Paul
carried with him one of the German individual field
radios. About the size of the Motorola units twentieth
century police officers carried, it attached to the belt,
wires traveling up along the torso. The wires ended in a
small vibration-sensitive unit which could transmit or
receive human speech, giving the unnerving feeling that
someone was alternately behind your back or reading
your mind.

Paul probably wasn't wearing it. Rourke activated
the radio. "This is John—come in, Paul. Do you read
me? Over."

There was nothing but static.

Paul was supposed to contact the gunship once he
reached the source of the smoke. They had agreed on
nothing else. Rourke's eyes moved once again to the
monitors. His right hand moved to his breast pocket,
extracted a cigar, the tip previously excised. He rolled
the cigar into the left side of his mouth, clamping down
on it with his teeth. "Paul—this is John. Do you read
me? Over."

They had agreed to maintain radio silence since, if
Paul found hostile personnel, the sound of an incoming
transmission, however slight, might be detected, might
betray him. John Rourke was beginning to think that
had been a bad idea. The black patches amid the bright
green leaves and stark whiteness of the snow were

black uniforms, men with assault rifles. The uniforms John Rourke instantly recognized: Soviet Marine Spetznas from the Soviet underwater complex.

"Shit," Rourke almost whispered. On the plus side, if they were on the island to begin with, they had to have a purpose which somehow likely involved Mid-Wake personnel. And to contact Mid-Wake personnel in order to secure help or information in the search for Annie and Natalia and Otto Hammerschmidt was the objective of the mission.

The gunship was ready to fly, able to be taken airborne in under sixty seconds. If he started the rotors so he could get airborne instantly, he could at the least alert the Marine Spetznas personnel observing the gunship, perhaps scare them off. With any luck, they had never seen a helicopter in the flesh before and wouldn't instantly identify its source or be one hundred percent certain what to do to a helicopter to immobilize it. It would be difficult for their small caliber rifles to immobilize the gunship at any event, unless a stray shot hit just the right place on just the right portion of the helicopter. Of course, there were always RPGs to consider, and Rourke had no idea, either, what the range of an Island Class submarine's deck guns might be.

The men in the black uniforms were moving, in a classic skirmish line, coming up from downstream only. If any more were hidden upstream or on either side of the shoals, Rourke could not see them.

Six men.

John Rourke found the battered Zippo in a side pants pocket, lit it, lit the cigar, inhaled.

Chances were very good these men had never seen a gunship in action, had no idea of its capabilities. Intrinsic to victory was knowledge of the enemy, weaknesses and strengths. Intrinsic to the communications system of the gunship was a public address capability. There was an obvious weakness he could exploit.

Mechanically he checked all systems, armed the helicopter's mini-guns.

The six men were moving just as they had been, approximately a hundred yards downstream from the gunship. One of them might notice the video cameras mounted beneath the main rotor following them. He doubted that.

Ninety yards.

Seventy-five yards.

He cut power to the helicopter's skin, killing all passive defense systems except video monitoring.

Mentally, John Thomas Rourke ticked off the seconds. If the pace of the Marine Spetznas personnel advancing against the machine remained constant, they were ninety seconds from the gunship's starboard fuselage door. What they had in mind to do when they reached it was another question.

"Eighty."

His eyes alternated between the sweep second hand of the black-faced Rolex Submariner on his left wrist and the instruments and the monitors.

"Seventy."

If anything, the six men were slowing their pace. Were they reluctant to approach out of a lack of knowledge of the machine's capabilities? He thought so.

"Sixty—" John Rourke powered up main and tail rotor controls, snow swirling around him in a gigantic cloud, momentarily obscuring the picture provided by the video cameras beneath the main rotor, the rotor blades humming as they built revolution, Rourke eyes on the pressure gauges, tachometers.

He was counting down seconds. "Fifty."

As Rourke's video returned, he could see the six Marine Spetznas personnel were scattering, one of them, evidently an officer or senior non-com, trying to rally the men.

"Thirty seconds." He tried the radio again. "Paul. This is John. Do you read me? If you cannot respond verbally, open and close transmission. Over."

Nothing.

"Fifteen seconds."

Almost enough power.

He checked the arming status on his weapons pods in case one of the enemy personnel had an RPG strapped on his back. Weapons pod, port starboard, fore and aft were armed.

Five seconds remained.

Power was adequate if he ate up seconds by spinning the machine on its axis, which would look forbidding to the Soviet personnel at any event—he hoped.

He let the gunship slip to port as it rose into the air, the helicopter turning a full 360 degrees, snow blowing beneath it cyclonically, the Soviet personnel hammered back by the force of wind-driven snow, gravel from the shoals, a spray of icy water as Rourke climbed, banked slightly, skipping rotor blade downdraft across the shoals.

Automatic weapons fire came at him, small arms only, none of it striking the skin.

Rourke rotated the gunship a full 360 degrees again, as he came on line with the Soviet personnel opening fire with starboard forward firing mini-guns, the bullets lacing across the shoals, across the snow, a long tongue of orange flame visible to him as his eyes shifted momentarily to the video displays.

The men began running downstream, slipping among the snow and ice-slicked rocks, John Rourke bringing the gunship's nose around, passing over them

146

low, a wash of water from the stream driven outward in a wake on both sides of the gunship, beating the Marine Spetznas personnel down.

For all their twenty-fifth century submarine technology, they seemed as frightened as Stone Age men by the flying machine which spit death, which ripped the water from the earth and hurtled it against them as if it were a wall.

He tried the radio again. "Paul. This is John. If you cannot respond because of an equipment failure, I just hope you can hear me. I'm airborne now, confronting six armed Marine Spetznas personnel on the ground at our landing site. I should shortly have them subdued and will obtain whatever information possible. I will then proceed along your probable route. Look for me. I'll be looking for you. After this, there's no sense trying to hide. These six likely have radio capability and are equally likely to have reported presence of the gunship. Rourke Out."

Rourke brought the German gunship out of the pass, banking to port, coming around, then cutting across the six Marine Spetznas' line of flight, blocking their retreat, more sporadic gunfire coming toward the gunship. Rourke felt the corners of his mouth raise in a smile as his teeth clamped on the lit cigar. The skin of the gunship could be charged again, as it had been before he'd switched off the defense systems package preparatory to going airborne.

He put power to the skin, then brought the gunship around, diving straight for them, following the stream bed, dropping altitude, increasing revolutions, streaking over them at maximum supportable speed for the altitude and surrounding terrain, the wall of water which rose on either side of the gunship reacting against the electrically charged hull, lightninglike bolts of electricity surrounding the gunship in a whirlwind,

147

the Marine Spetznas personnel scattering, throwing themselves toward the bands of the shallow stream.

Rourke cut power to the skin, then hovered the craft over the Marine Spetznas personnel. They cowered beneath the gunship, the downdraft visibly tearing at their uniforms.

In his best, most menacing Russian, John Rourke told them, "Your weapons are useless; you are powerless to resist." He assumed somehow that they had never viewed the same classic B-movie science fiction thrillers he had.

Chapter Twenty-Four

"Sam—have a few of your men lay back and cover us."

"You heard the Captain—you, you—Lannigan. You're in charge. Take 'em up into those rocks and cover us. Shoot anything in a Soviet uniform."

"Yes, sir!" And Lannigan gestured to both men, got them moving.

Jason Darkwood stood at the foot of a chimney of rock. It was colder here in the higher elevations. There was evidence of much recent volcanic activity, at least geologically recent. Marine geology was part of the standard curriculum since Mid-Wake depended for its minerals on mining the sea, and for its energy on geo-thermal faults. Surface geology seemed little different to him. He had climbed rock chimneys in underwater caves in full diving gear back in his academy days and since, for real purposes. He supposed, if anything, it might be easier doing it in more conventional attire on land.

Evidently, the Marine Spetznas personnel who were now their prisoners had not come quite this way. More than he had ever realized before, Mid-Wake personnel desperately needed training in surface warfare, simply reading the terrain a vital skill. When one essentially flew over the terrain by swimming, it wasn't as necessary to be conscious of it.

Darkwood looked at the Marine Spetznas prisoners. The Soviets had a decided advantage. Under similar circumstances, if the prisoners were not valuable to the Soviets they would have been drugged nearly out of their minds and bound, then left to freeze to death in the snow if it came to that, he supposed. Either that or killed outright.

But the citizens of Mid-Wake labored under a different moral imperative. And, despite the inconvenience at the moment, he would not have abandoned that. It was this moral imperative which lay as the foundation of his beliefs and those of his comrades and all citizens of Mid-Wake. He supposed it was this moral imperative which made Americans the "good guys." Darkwood looked at his old friend Captain Sam Aldridge, U.S.M.C. "So—just how many guys do we leave to guard our six unhappy Russian friends?"

Aldridge detailed four men, leaving them with instructions to shoot anyone who moved without permission, then reiterating those instructions in Russian for the benefit of the prisoners.

Darkwood nominated himself to go first, up the rock chimney. He unslung his pack and cinched the sling of his AKM-96 up tightly, then squeezed through, Aldridge handing the pack in after him. The rock seemed to radiate cold. Darkwood told himself that was psychological. He looked up. The chimney rose for perhaps seventy-five feet. All his climbing experience was in the water, except for climbing trees and things as a boy in the Mid-Wake nature preserves. In water, there was buoyancy and buoyancy compensation, the force of gravity partially neutralized by buoyancy. He told himself that, if he fell, he'd really get the feel for gravity here.

Although the conditions were different, the technique would be the same, he realized. He snapped the end of his rope into his pack, then attached the other end to his belt, leaving the coil beside the pack, so he could haul the pack up after him. He braced himself inside the chimney, his right leg up, his left hand pressured, his left leg and right hand up. Right leg, left hand; left leg, right hand; he repeated the process over and over again, not looking down at all until the chimney began narrowing. The narrowing was an advantage. He could use more body surface against the chimney walls, making himself at least feel more secure and actually speeding his progress. He was tiring more quickly than he would have underwater, he realized. He stopped, approximately halfway up the chimney, catching his breath before going on . . .

Paul Rubenstein found a gently sloping, easy path toward the promontory at the height of the ridgeline, from which the column of gray smoke originated.

There was a breadloaf-shaped rock sitting on a shelf of rock extending toward a plateau which appeared recently made from a volcanic flow. As a boy, he'd liked geology well enough to become reasonably conversant in the field—in more than one school science fair he'd used rock collections, this made all the easier because his Air Force officer father would be transferred to a different base and the new school hadn't seen the rock collection the previous year. But his mother always made him do something new with it. His father. His mother. Like uncounted millions of others, they had died during the Great Conflagration, when the sky caught fire and nearly all surface life ceased.

What would they think of him now? They had been proud of him— He shook his head, forced his thoughts away from his memories. They would have loved Annie, her being a Gentile notwithstanding.

As he approached the peculiarly shaped rock, it was apparent there were two ways to get to the other side, over or around. Over it looked needlessly time-consuming and, because of the snow, dangerous.

He walked around it, the M-16 in his right fist, the Schmiesser submachine gun in his left. He laughed at himself, feeling like Stallone or Schwarzenegger or Norris in some pre-Night of the War adventure film. That he didn't look like any of them no longer really bothered him. He'd learned that rippling muscles weren't a requirement for derring-do; but, granted, they would have helped at times. He kept moving.

There was a peculiar odor to the smoke, something he had smelled before; but he couldn't remember when. The wind shifted and the odor was gone. Paul Rubenstein walked on, the column of smoke completely gone from sight now, the breadloaf-shaped rock between him and its source. A signal fire? It certainly had attracted a considerable amount of attention. Perhaps all of this was nothing more than a group of stranded Russian seamen lighting a signal fire because they were marooned. Paul Rubenstein tried imagining the Defoe classic with a Communist flavor. Comrade Friday? At least Comrade Crusoe would be good alliteration. There had been a variation on *Robinson Crusoe* done as a film he'd seen as a little boy, the film set on Mars in some distant future. The landscape here looked more appropriate to that, stark, forbidding.

Paul Rubenstein reached the extreme end of the breadloaf-shaped rock.

He dropped to his knees, murmuring, "God of Abraham!" Tears filled his eyes . . .

*   *   *

Six assault rifles, an assortment of individual weapons, two RPGs. Rourke climbed, using the public address and warning the Marine Spetznas personnel below the German gunship, "Get back from your weapons or you, too, will be destroyed."

The six men, including their non-com, ran. Rourke had cornered them, gotten them to disarm, never landed, never interrogated them. It seemed pointless to waste a missile destroying their weapons. Instead, he let the chopper turn 180 degrees on its axis, flew off and climbed, banked to port and dived, activating port and starboard forward mini-guns, the twin bursts ripping across the pile of Soviet armament, the RPGs exploding as Rourke banked to starboard and climbed.

He oriented himself toward the column of smoke, flew toward it, looking for signs of Paul below him . . .

At last, Jason Darkwood reached the height of the chimney. He could smell the smoke very strongly. There was something faintly sweet and faintly nauseating about it as he climbed out.

He looked across a barren, volcanic rock flat. "Jesus." Jason Darkwood could do nothing but stare, his throat tightening as he tried to fight back tears.

Chapter Twenty-Five

Annie Rubenstein sat in a comfortable chair, her legs curled up almost under her. She reached toward Maggie Barrow's desk, took the small cup, and sipped at her tea.

"Do you faint very often?"

"No."

"Were you seeing what was going on in Major Tiemerovna's thoughts, Annie?"

"Maybe—I think so," she told Maggie Barrow.

"And that made you faint?"

"Yes. I guess so."

"What was it that you saw, Annie?"

"My father's face—just coming in and out and disappearing and reappearing—there were flames and—"

"And so that—" Maggie Barrow began again.

"No," Annie interrupted. "Daddy always wears these aviator-style sunglasses, with real dark lenses. He must have a couple of dozen pair of them at the Retreat. He's very light-sensitive; he always has been. And when the light hits them just right, you can see things in the lenses. Like a reflection. I used to like to look at myself in them when I was a little girl. But this time, I saw what Natalia was seeing in the glasses."

"What was that, Annie?"

"It was a skull, a skull in each of the lenses. Like death. That's what I saw."

Maggie Barrow folded her hands around her right knee as she sat on the edge of the desk, crossed her legs. "There's a man at Mid-Wake. A very fine man. A great man. His name is Rothstein, Doctor Phillip Rothstein. He's a psychiatrist, but so much more than that. I saw him do something once. Where he hypnotized somebody. Well, I was thinking, what if he hypnotized you and helped you to clear your mind so you could—well, like you say it—so you could enter Major Tiemerovna's mind? Unless I miss my guess, as long as she's so deeply into the depressive stage she's in that she remains catatonic, unless she can be brought out of it with drugs, how can anyone really help her? But, if you were able to probe Major Tiemerovna's mind, he could—"

"My mind would be like a monitor for him to use."

"Doctor Rothstein might not want to—it might be too dangerous for you," Maggie Barrow said.

Annie Rubenstein looked at her, sipped at the tea. "I'll try it; she'd do the same for me. If she hadn't helped my father, none of us would be alive. When can we talk to this Doctor Rothstein?"

Maggie Barrow didn't answer, just looked through the open office door. Annie's eyes tracked after her gaze. Natalia moved restlessly in a drug-induced sleep, her body bound to the bed with restraints so she could not hurt herself.

Natalia was unable to do anything for herself, was dead while still alive. Annie told herself that Paul would understand why she had to do this thing Doctor Barrow had brought up. And if Doctor Rothstein at Mid-Wake didn't want to help, then perhaps Doctor

Munchen could find a similar specialist in New Germany. But just thinking of it, she felt like a thief waiting to strike. The mind was the repository of hopes and dreams, secret longings and nightmares—and they were Natalia's private things, personal things and did anyone have the right to look at them without her permission? But unless she miraculously snapped out of this, or there were some possible cure Maggie Barrow wasn't aware of, what then? Leave Natalia to spend weeks or months, years, perhaps the rest of her life like she was now? Or look into those secret things in secret places?

And Annie Rourke Rubenstein shivered, because she knew she would find her father there and Marshal Karamatsov and the Night of the War, all of it in reality and fantasy and in ways she did not want to consider because they frightened her.

Chapter Twenty-Six

There was no sign of Paul from above as Rourke followed the ridgeline toward the summit which was the source of the column of smoke. He followed the terrain with the machine to avoid making it easier for the Island Classer to track him if indeed it had such capabilities at all. There was no doubt in his mind that someone from the party of six Marine Spetznas personnel he'd herded together and forced to disarm had alerted the vessel prior to moving in.

As John Rourke brought the gunship over the ridgeline, he saw the source of the smoke. Surrounding it were a group of men, some in black uniforms that could have been Marine Spetznas or Mid-Wake. From the altitude, he couldn't be certain. But standing with them, clearly, was Paul Rubenstein. They formed a ragged semicircle around the remains of a huge bonfire. But there were no trees anywhere on the plateaulike slab of volcanic rock and to have hauled wood to the center of the barren rock rather than set the fire nearer to the ridgeline where there was timber closer at hand seemed—

John Rourke's hand froze on the stick, a sudden dry feeling in his mouth. He circled, the smoke dissipating in his downdraft, Paul Rubenstein waving him in.

"This can't be," Rourke almost whispered.

He let the gunship settle over the plateau, slipping to port and down, leaving power to his main rotor.

Walking toward him from the origin of the smoke was Paul Rubenstein, and beside him a tall, lean, dark curly-haired man, but the usual grin on the man's face gone, his face and Paul's face wearing almost the same expression.

Rourke hit the release for his seat restraint, went to the fuselage door, opened it, dropped down into the snow, not bothering with a coat, his breath steaming, the wind cutting through his black knit shirt like a knife.

"John—"

"Doctor Rourke—it's—"

John Rourke bit down hard on his cigar.

He walked ahead, the wind tearing at his hair, his fingers pushing it back from his forehead.

He walked between Paul Rubenstein and Jason Darkwood, toward the bonfire.

"John—"

John Rourke didn't answer.

The smell of the smoke.

Twisted, contorted shapes, still smoldering, blunted curves, upthrusting angles, as if reaching—

Paul shouted on the wind. "John—they're people."

John Rourke turned away from the smoke.

Chapter Twenty-Seven

Vassily Prokopiev listened to the clicking of his own bootheels as he walked along the otherwise empty corridor toward the double doors at its end. It was too early for anyone, even in a predominantly military society such as that of the Underground City.

He stopped at the doors, gave a last look to his boots, a last tug to his uniform tunic, then opened the right-hand door, his uniform cap under his left arm.

No secretary sat at the outer office desk and only a single lamp at the head of the desk was turned on, illuminating the green blotter with a yellow wash. He closed the door behind him.

"Major—is that you?" It was the voice of Comrade Colonel Antonovitch, coming from the inner office.

"Yes, Comrade Colonel," Prokopiev called back, approaching the inner office door.

Here no overhead lights shone either, but two lamps were lit, one on each side of the desk and several feet away from it, one on each side of the picture of Lenin.

"Have you ever been in this office before, Vassily?" The Comrade Colonel's chair was turned with the back facing toward the connecting doorway in which Prokopiev stood.

161

"Once, Comrade Colonel."

"Then you will not blame me for the choice of decor." As he spoke, the chair swung around 180 degrees and Colonel Antonovitch leaned forward across the littered desk, hands locking together as his fingers intertwined. "The Hero Marshal, as Vladmir Karamatsov liked having himself called, had strange tastes. That terrible picture of Nicolai Lenin and yet the frame is plated with genuine gold. And the bar. One would have thought that our Hero Marshal was planning for another five centuries of survival, only this time awake. At least to start with. Come in. And close the door behind you."

Prokopiev walked across the room, stopped a meter from the desk, and came to attention.

"Stand easy—take a seat. Vassily—" and the Comrade Colonel shook his head. "I don't really know what to do with you. I mean, I know what I must do. But— I read your report concerning the destruction of the Second Chinese City, concerning the evacuation from their missile silo or temple."

Prokopiev felt he was not interrupting. "It was both, Comrade Colonel."

"They are calling me 'Marshal' these days."

"Comrade Marshal."

"Why did you include the information concerning John Rourke and Michael Rourke and their Jewish comrade, this Rubenstein fellow?"

"I felt, Comrade Colonel—Comrade Marshal. I felt that I should make an honest report."

Comrade—Comrade Marshal Antonovitch raised his head, smiled. "You have shown me that I am perhaps a better military commander than I might have supposed, Vassily. I desired to pick the best man possible, the best officer available to head the Elite Corps. And, from among the KGB elite corps, seeking

162

a truly honorable man can be a frustrating task. But, it appears in you that I have indeed found such a man. But, unfortunately, Vassily, you are also a fool. What would our late Hero Marshal have done to a member of the KGB Elite Corps who had several opportunities to kill John Thomas Rourke and did not?"

"I—I do not—"

"You know. Killing would have been too merciful." And the Comrade Marshal laughed softly. "He might have eaten such a hapless person. Who knows? He was an animal. No wonder his wife left him for another man, if indeed she did. No. I would tear up this report of yours," and he raised a file folder from the litter of his desktop, fanned it for a moment, let it tumble from his hand to the desk, the papers inside spilling out. "But I cannot because, by now, the Chairman has a copy of this report. He will demand your arrest and trial and execution for treason. And I can do nothing to stop him. But, you knew that when you composed your report."

"Yes, Comrade Marshal."

"And still you wrote what you did."

"Yes, Comrade Marshal. There is a trust I cannot violate."

The Comrade Marshal looked at him, smiled, shook his head. "I don't suppose you are the sort of man who would choose suicide? Death before dishonor, certainly but not suicide in a situation such as this."

"That is correct, Comrade Marshal."

"And, what will you say at your trial, Vassily?"

"Comrade Marshal?"

"When you are asked why you, a Major of the Elite Corps, its commander, why you allowed this wanted war criminal to go free, along with several other war criminals. Why did you?"

"Comrade—Comrade Marshal," Prokopiev began,

realizing he was stammering. "He, ahh— His son saved my life. Doctor Rourke is a man of consummate bravery. He could not be the evil person he has been painted to be. I spoke with him. I fought beside him. He— Perhaps—"

"The Hero Marshal, our courageous, honorable, and always truthful Vladimir Karamatsov lied? See how far you get saying such a thing at a trial."

"But—"

"Your wounds. You seem fit enough."

"I will be—" There was no point in saying that he would be fine, recover perfectly. He had known his fate as he had begun the first word of his report, sealed that fate with his signature.

"You will be dead, Vassily. Let me ask you a question. Who do you think is right?"

"Comrade Marshal?"

"I asked, Who do you think is morally right? Ourselves, or our enemies?"

"The Soviet people—"

"Now, Vassily—I said nothing about the Soviet people. I meant, based upon your experiences, who do you think is right? Is our side, the side of global Communism, correct. Or—whatever Doctor Rourke's side could be described as. Is he correct. Is his side correct? What do you think?"

"The Soviet people are—"

"'—the finest and most courageous people.' Yes, I know that. I speak philosophy, not of the people."

Vassily Prokopiev felt as if he were twelve years old and confronted by his schoolmaster. "I—"

"You cannot get in any trouble, which could possibly be worse, Vassily."

Prokopiev nodded, looked at his hands, at his feet, up into the Comrade Marshal's oddly sympathetic-looking face. "I have come to believe that perhaps many things told to me as true might well be lies, or distortions of the truth at least."

"You are remarkably astute. And?"

"Comrade Marshal?"

"Armed with this knowledge, what is your intention, if somehow you should survive?"

"I do not—"

"Well, let me enlighten you further," the Comrade Marshal said, his voice low, strange sounding. "Before what your newfound friends refer to as the Night of the War, The United States and The Union of Soviet Socialist Republics were moving toward mutual nuclear disarmament. There were certain factions within both countries, in fairness, which felt that such a policy was disaster, each distrusting the other, fearing the other, fearing weakness in themselves. And some who lusted for power and saw a war footing as the means by which to preserve existing power and increase their power. The Hero Marshal Karamatsov worked tirelessly, tirelessly I say—tirelessly to bring about global destruction on a scale never before possible. There is a poem you will not have read, not have heard of, by a poet whose name you will not know. He was English. John Milton. The poem spoke of the Judeo-Christian myth of Paradise, and is entitled *Paradise Lost*. In this poem, the devil—the Judeo-Christian personification of ultimate evil as opposed to God, ultimate good—declares that he would rather rule in Hell than serve in Heaven. And this, apparently, was the guiding principle of the Hero Marshal, back in the days when he was a Colonel in the KGB, when he worked in what was then Latin America, in the Middle East, in the very United States itself.

"Karamatsov," Comrade Marshal Antonovitch went on, "set about to turn the Earth into a hell over which he could rule. Where there was distrust, he wanted

165

hatred. Where there was the potential for violent up-heaval, he wanted war. He—and to be fair, others like him—succeeded. Which is why you and I are contem-poraries. I served under him in those days, saw his evil, did nothing. After he was shot down by John Rourke, I was one of those who brought him here, used the criogenic sleep as a means of suspending death while all around us for five centuries there was birth and death and deprivation in between.

"I know of what I speak," Comrade Marshal Antonovitch concluded.

"I knew that you were one of—"

"His original disciples? Yes. I saw something here. A Chairman who seeks war as desperately as Vladimir Karamatsov sought it. A woman who slept with me because she wished to use me as a means of promoting this war. You must understand me," the Comrade Marshal said, rising and standing behind his desk, looking down on Prokopiev as if for emphasis. "I sought the missiles of the Second Chinese City, I launched the global offensive. But I did all of this and will continue as Marshal of the Soviet Union, because I sought what used to be called a 'Pax Romana.' During the reign of Augustus Caesar in the old Roman Empire thousands of years ago, there was almost universal peace because there was almost universal government. My goal was to end war with war, not to risk the end of mankind. While someone else controlled the nuclear arsenal of prewar China, there was the chance that it might be used, as Karamatsov had planned to use it. But now, the Chairman seeks to contact our supposed Comrades beneath the sea, the antagonists of the Americans at Mid-Wake. He wishes to use their nuclear submarines and nuclear missiles. He has authorized the redevelopment of our twentieth century particle beam device with which Karamatsov and

166

Rozhdestvenskiy after him, when it was thought Karamatsov was dead, intended to destroy the Eden Project and establish clearly total Soviet rule. Rozhdestvenskiy, according to documents unearthed by our archaeological teams at Cheyenne Mountain in American Colorado where the Womb, our retreat, our own KGB Underground City was to have been before Rourke destroyed it, personally ordered the deaths of ranking Soviet officials coming to the Womb for their own survival. Rozhdestvenskiy did this in order to assure his own power. The particle beam technology is now so advanced that these weapons can be mounted on armored vehicles, in helicopter gunships, made in any size or power range. Soon, they will be adapted as infantry machine guns. No conventional weapon except nuclear weapons will stand against these. With the nuclear potential of the Soviet civilization beneath the sea and the particle beam technology, all resistance will be destroyed. There will be an Empire of Death. If the Earth is not totally destroyed when the first nuclear weapon is utilized—and the Germans of New Germany in Argentina are developing nuclear weapons for their defense—the Soviet people will be the only people who will survive, but they will survive to live under the most despotic rule in human history. And still, there will be no peace. Will the Chairman surrender authority to the nuclear-capable new Comrades after their enemies at Mid-Wake and our enemies have all been destroyed? I think he will not. Instead, there will be war again. It will never end until the Earth ends."

Prokopiev watched the Comrade Marshal's eyes. "Why do you tell me this, Comrade Marshal?"

"You are in a unique position." And suddenly a pistol appeared in Antonovitch's right hand, almost as if he had pulled it from thin air. It was very small, and likely very old. "This is a .25 caliber Beretta, in answer to your unspoken question. It is almost as old as I am. You are here because you are an honorable man, honorable to the point of willingly surrendering your life because it is the morally correct thing to do. I wish for you to leave me with this in your pocket." And the Comrade Marshal produced a small object about the size of the spool of thread Prokopiev kept in his kit for the resewing of buttons. "There is film inside this canister. The film contains the plans for the particle beam devices which will soon be used in the field against the allies of Doctor Rourke. Make no mistake, Vassily. I am a loyal Communist. I shall continue to defend the Soviet people to the best of my ability. But my answer, I have realized—and it has taken me five centuries to come to this realization—my answer is not the best answer. Will you serve the Soviet people and all people?"

"How, Comrade Marshal?"

"Doctor Rourke is a man like yourself, a man of honor. And, it would appear from your report, so is his son. Give this film to him and tell him that I trust he will do the right thing. Will you take it?"

"How can—"

"You are the most highly trained man in the Elite Corps. I cannot believe you could not find a way, Vassily."

Prokopiev cleared his throat, looked at his hands. They trembled slightly. "Yes, Comrade Marshal."

The Comrade Marshal tossed the canister across the desk, Prokopiev watching it come toward him somehow as if it were in slow motion. He caught it in his right hand. His hand no longer trembled.

"I have two messages for you. Tell Comrade Major Tiemerovna that perhaps she was right about me after all. She always told me that I was not born to Karamatsov's work."

"Two messages, Comrade Marshal?"

"Yes. Tell Doctor Rourke this changes nothing. I would kill him if I had the chance. And I will expect the same courtesy from him. There is a pack, there are winter clothes, there is a fine knife, there is a pistol, an assault rifle and adequate ammunition, foodstuffs and personal medical supplies. Do what you must. If you take a life from within the Elite Corps, it will be one less to hunt you down and kill you. Remember that Communism, if it is good, is to serve the people. Living people. Now take the film, guard it against any sort of radiation. Take this pistol and shoot me in the arm with it. In the fleshy part—here."

He set the pistol on the desk, then touched at his outer left forearm.

Prokopiev picked up the pistol. It was very small. "The hammer is already cocked, Vassily," the Comrade Marshal advised. "The gun shoots true at short range. There is little muzzle blast. We fought over the gun, of course; you took it and attempted to kill me, but I shoved you away and that deflected your bullet. The safety catch is on the left-hand side. Push it down. Watch for the web of your hand as you shoot. It is a very small gun. Shoot me."

Vassily Prokopiev raised the pistol, took a single step, hesitated, then took another step back. He aimed the pistol—it had very rudimentary sights—at the Comrade Marshal's outstretched left arm. His thumb found the safety catch and he pushed it down as instructed. Why would anyone wish a gun so small?

"Yes, Comrade Marshal." Vassily Prokopiev pulled the trigger and the Comrade Marshal fell back against the picture of Lenin, clasping his left forearm. The Comrade Marshal smiled.

Chapter Twenty-Eight

It was necessary, after trying to connect the pieces as best as possible, to rope the dead down through the rock chimney. A mass grave would have been impossible to dig on the volcanic flow. One hundred and twenty men were detailed to the surface warfare group on Iwo Jima. The remains of as many as fifty—at least there were fifty skulls that could be found—were in the giant bonfire, parts of it still reeking of something which smelled like gasoline and which the men of Mid-Wake identified as something which sounded to be the Soviet equivalent of napalm.

There were the remains of plastic ropes, not fully burned, and there was no evidence any of the men had been shot before being set afire. The evidence, on the contrary, seemed clear that the men were executed in the flames, by the flames.

Once their bodies were roped down, the grave was dug. No one suggested that the six Soviet prisoners should be used to assist. It would have seemed, Paul Rubenstein reflected, to dishonor the dead.

John Rourke interrogated the six Soviet prisoners. The remaining survivors of the attack on Iwo Jima were being transported—walked—through the jungle, stripped of their uniforms (hence freezing), toward the

Island Class submarine anchored off the island. They would be taken by the Soviets for "scientific experiments." The Soviet undersea colony had been practicing surface warfare for the last decade, been aware of the Iwo Jima facility for six months at least, decided to leave a message for the people of Mid-Wake, one they would never forget.

Paul Rubenstein agreed with that; the message would never be forgotten.

"We have two choices," John Rourke said, Paul Rubenstein watching him as he, John Rourke, Jason Darkwood, and Sam Aldridge walked toward the helicopter gunship, the six Soviet prisoners and the rest of Aldridge's Marines waiting uneasily near the rock chimney. The Soviet prisoners had to be terrified that they would be executed in like manner to the Americans from Mid-Wake, or worse. And the Marines had to be tempted.

Captain—formerly Commander—Jason Darkwood asked, "Are they the same two choices I'm thinking of, Doctor Rourke?"

"I would imagine they are," John nodded.

"With your daughter, Mrs. Rubenstein, and Major Tiemerovna and Captain Hammerschmidt safe, you and your flying machine are capable of pursuing other interests."

"That's right, Captain," John agreed. "Revenge sounds like a good start."

"Can this—this gunship," and Darkwood gestured toward the German craft, "destroy an Island Classer, Doctor?"

"With a great deal of luck, yes. Although I know what the German missiles will do against Soviet surface armor, I have no idea what they'll do against a double hull capable of withstanding the depths these vessels routinely sustain. With a great deal of luck, yes—I can probably destroy it. Or, with a little assistance and less

172

luck, I know I can destroy it. We'll have to free the prisoners first, of course. Have to free them so that if we do get the Island Classer to blow, when she does their captors won't automatically massacre them. And we'll have to do it very quickly—the rescue, I mean—so they won't have time to radio the Island Classer that we're getting them. The Island Classer knows about the helicopter, but probably has very little understanding of its capabilities. At best, computer records might give a breakdown of the abilities of late twentieth-century helicopter gunships. This German version is vastly quicker, more maneuverable, better, and more heavily armed. They couldn't expect that, at least not without some good minds going to work on it, and there won't have been time for that, either."

John stopped beneath the now-still blades of the main rotor. "Now," he continued. "I think we have a chance. The six men you took prisoner are the key. From your account, Captain, of their capture, they couldn't possibly have radioed in their predicament. Therefore, they're still expected. Even considering the time we spent in the burial, we can get them to the right spot using the helicopter, making up for the lost time."

"Get us, you mean," Jason Darkwood said.

Sam Aldridge smiled. "We put on their uniforms, walk right up to them."

"No—that suntan routine worked the last time, Sam," Darkwood said. "You control the second element, for the ambush."

Paul Rubenstein spoke. "Assuming we get the rest of the Mid-Wake personnel free—what, seventy or so?"

"Aside from casualties," Captain Aldridge interjected, his voice low. "They might have been heavy. Probably were. Most of the people here were Marines."

"Then assuming we get them free," Paul continued, "what if we salvage as many additional uniforms as possible, then walk the Mid-Wake personnel aboard the Island Class submarine. Instead of you blowing it, John, why not take it?"

John Rourke turned and looked at him. "That's very simple, very brilliant, Paul."

"No U.S. skipper has boarded a major enemy vessel during an action since the U-505 submarine during World War Two," Jason Darkwood murmured. "I mean, that Island Classer we hijacked wasn't manned, wasn't—"

Darkwood referred to the vessel he and Sam Aldridge and a handful of Marine raiders had stolen during their rescue of Natalia from Mid-Wake. Aldridge interrupted Paul's thoughts. "Well, don't forget that little scout sub my people took. But you're right, Jase."

"How's that Island Class submarine you and your men took doing, anyway?" John Rourke asked, smiling.

"Well, now that you bring it up," Jason Darkwood smiled back, "I understand it's getting very lonely for one of its own kind. In a way, we'd be performing a humanitarian act. Not to mention probably netting ourselves a full complement of Soviet missiles, too."

Paul Rubenstein watched as John Rourke turned away from the gunship and stared back toward where the six prisoners were. "That Soviet Marine Spetznas Sergeant. He's a big one. That might be why he didn't give in entirely to the truth drug. Or maybe he really had no knowledge of the burning of the prisoners and couldn't tell us. At least I can hope. It wouldn't be convincing to put someone into his uniform. And anyway, the blood stains on the other uniforms weren't so bad. I think it will just have to be five of us. You, Captain, Paul here, myself and two other of your men." John Rourke lit the partially burned stump of cigar, shielding the flame of his Zippo against the wind in his cupped palms.

Chapter Twenty-Nine

Falling, blowing snow swirled in kaleidoscopic patterns in the light.

Michael Rourke's flashlight showed solid rock. But Bjorn Rolvaag tapped him on the shoulder and gestured that they should move ahead. Michael switched off the flashlight and followed him.

The snow which seemed to fall everywhere according to the German meteorological reports was a blizzard here. Michael Rourke doubted that even with Rolvaag's expertise in Arctic travel and survival and the aid of his dog, Hrothgar, they would be able to go on much farther, nor certainly be able to turn back.

Maria was roped behind him, Michael following Rolvaag, Maria and the German commandos and volunteers from the German Hekla Base following him.

Somehow, the dog would be there one instant and gone into the blizzard the next, totally lost from sight, only then returning to run off once more.

It crossed Michael's mind that perhaps Rolvaag's head injury had been more serious than anyone considered, that he was simply leading them on into the blizzard out of delusion. Michael Rourke could feel

Maria Leuden beside him, feel the pressure of her heavily gloved hands on his left forearm. He folded his arm around her, trudged ahead, the snowdrifts at times waist-high, the temperature so cold that his thighs, despite the several layers of thermal clothing, were stiffening, his legs almost refusing to move. He kept going.

Bjorn Rolvaag was a man who was driven, clearly. Every instinct in Rolvaag's body must have been telling him to press on, to find this tunnel whether it existed or not, penetrate the tunnel, reach the interior of the Hekla cone and rush to the rescue of his country's leader, Madame Jokli.

Every instinct. Michael hoped they were real, rather than delusion.

Maria Leuden was shouting something and Michael could not distinguish the words. He pushed his hood back on the left side, a sudden shock of cold as he opened it, leaned his toqued and scarfed head toward her completely covered mouth. He thought he made out the words, "I will die, Michael!" He held her more tightly, kept moving. Turning back would have been pointless. Where was back?

Michael kept moving, slamming into what felt like a wall. It was Bjorn Rolvaag, swathed in his furs, Hrothgar bounding back and forth in the cone of Michael's flashlight as, once again, he turned it on. There was no chance that the Russian occupation forces might have had sentries at the height of the cone who could have seen the light. Visibility was nearly measurable in inches, certainly only in feet.

Rolvaag pointed into the darkness beyond the snow which swirled in Michael's light, then started toward—what? Michael saw nothing. Rolvaag kept moving, Michael in his wake, dragging Maria now almost, ready to take her up into his arms and carry her because he realized she could go no farther, really. If they were attacked now, even assuming they could tell from which direction, he doubted his M-16's bolt could be cleared of ice quickly enough to fire back. His other weapons were beneath his parka, hopeless to get to, his hands numb and stiff.

Michael Rourke kept walking.

Rock— He slammed into it, stumbled, dragging Maria Leuden down into the snow with him. But as he reached out, there was nothing there. He swept his hand right and left. To the right, there was solidness.

Michael pulled himself to his knees, to his feet, spoke to Maria, knowing she couldn't hear him over the keening of the wind. "I think it's the tunnel, Maria."

He pulled her to her feet, feeling the forward pressure of Rolvaag's rope tugging him ahead.

He took a step, then another and another, then another and then—then the snow stopped and the howl of the wind was like the howl of the sea in a shell. He'd heard that as a little boy.

One of the lanterns was lit, moved. In the light from it, he could see Rolvaag's face. There was no snow around his face. They were inside the tunnel.

Bjorn Rolvaag's great lionine face seamed with a fine smile.

Chapter Thirty

Since it was Colonel Mann's personal J7-V, the aircraft was furnished rather differently from the others in which she had flown, Sarah Rourke observed. His J7-V, for example, although a fighter craft, had a complete radio room in the rear of the fuselage. She gathered it was for more than ordinary radio. More likely, sophisticated electronic intelligence equipment racks.

He emerged from that room now, his face looking sad. She liked him very much as a person, as a friend. He treated her as a person and friend. And she liked that very much.

"Frau Rourke—Sarah. Your friend, Lieutenant Kurinami. He is now listed as officially missing in action and presumed dead. The men whose lives he saved have personally conducted an air search, had to turn back because of the storms raging in the southeastern United States and because of significant and growing Soviet presence. Nothing was seen of him. I hate to be the bearer of such news, Sarah."

Sarah Rourke stared out the cabin window of the J7-V.

"Wolf—would you try something? For me?"

He sat down opposite her, leaning toward her, his hands near her coffee cup. "If I can, of course."

"When Akiro and Elaine Halversen—his fiancée? When they escaped from Commander Dodd before, they went to the Retreat. I wouldn't feel as if everything had been done if somehow we didn't go there, make an aerial search of the surrounding area if possible, go to the Retreat itself. He could be there, perhaps injured or dying. It's worth a chance, isn't it, Wolfgang?"

Wolfgang Mann nodded, slowly, then said, "Yes—it is worth a chance. The aerial search may prove impossible. But we can try. And if the pilot is not willing to try a landing, I will—unless it would mean the deaths of all aboard. Yes." And he looked at his watch. "We won't be over northeastern Georgia for better than forty minutes. Then we will know. So sleep, now. I can get a blanket for you."

"Thank you," she nodded, her eyes very tired. "Where are we now—about, I mean?"

"We passed over the St. Lawrence River not long ago. I imagine we are somewhere near where your New York City once was." She looked into the darkness, imagining they were flying over New York City. Her New York City. That made her smile. But there would have been lights, beautiful lights. She was sure she could have seen them through the snow she knew was falling below them. She was sure.

But now, there was just darkness.

She turned her face more toward the window so he wouldn't see her cry, her fingers massaging at the life in her abdomen. A little boy. Another John? Another Michael? More fodder for a history likely no one would ever survive to read?

The tears flowed freely now and she hadn't thought that Wolfgang Mann was still watching her, but he whispered, "May I?" As he placed his arm around her

180

shoulders, held her tightly enough to be reassuring, comforting, not tightly enough that it would be misinterpreted. Sarah Rourke realized what she was. A widow with a living husband.

And she was very lonely.

When she closed her eyes tightly against the tears, she could see the lights.

Chapter Thirty-One

Vassily Prokopiev knew the Underground City. He was born there, raised there in the communal center for boys who had shown aptitude for military service. At age fourteen, he was transferred from the general military studies program to the special program, which of course was for the KGB. With the special program came a special school.

The curriculum was very demanding, from code-breaking skills to marksmanship to interrogation improvisations to chemical composition of poisons and explosives. And always, physical training. But, if studies went well and discipline was maintained, each boy had his day.

Prokopiev always applied himself to his studies, whether he perceived the specific subject matter as boring or exciting, useful or absurd; and one afternoon and early evening each weekend was his.

Sharp looking in his gray uniform, black boots, and black belt and his cap, he would move about the Underground City, watching of course for pretty girls, hoping they were watching back. The prettiest girls seemed to be those from the musical studies or dancing, but sometimes a surprisingly pretty girl would be found in the oddest place—loading sacks of grain, learning how to artificially inseminate one of the precious farm animals, driving a delivery truck.

Some of the boys at the academy where he studied were not at all interested in girls. At school, at night, it was sometimes necessary to watch out for them. He had studied hand-to-hand combat ever since he'd first shown military aptitude, but it was one night when he was still fifteen that he was in his first real fight. Some of those boys who did not like girls had decided that they were interested in him. He was not interested in them. Four of them. Only him and his boyhood friend Ivan against them. Ivan died years later during a training exercise when he was still very young. Ivan had never been strong, really, but that night, Ivan fought well.

He and Ivan had taken their afternoon off and gotten chocolate with money both of them had saved, then strolled about the streets of the Underground City. Everything always looked the same, but it was something to do, of course. And there were always the girls to look at, who never looked the same, like beautiful flowers somehow growing out of a slab of concrete.

But then Boris and his three friends came upon Prokopiev and his friend Ivan in the service alley behind the Cultural Arts Center. He and Ivan always cut through the service alley because it was quicker to the Youth Hall where there were always girls. Apparently, Boris had calculated their path and decided to lay in wait there with his three friends, all of them like Boris, all of them.

The attack came so quickly. Poor Ivan was struck in the throat with a paving stone and fell to the street, gasping for breath. Prokopiev himself was hit, but only in the arm, not so badly as Ivan certainly.

184

And Boris and his three friends swarmed over them, metal truncheons in their hands, really verticals pried out of the fence surrounding the Youth Hall. Prokopiev struck Boris twice in the face with his fists and Boris began to shriek with pain. Two of Boris's friends brought Prokopiev down. Boris was holding his bleeding nose and screaming at Prokopiev, calling Prokopiev every obscenity a fifteen-year-old could possibly know, waving the steel truncheon.

But suddenly, there was Ivan. Ivan kicked Boris in the groin and Boris fell to his knees. Prokopiev finished the job by kicking Boris in the face. And then Ivan fell on one of the two who held Prokopiev down, Prokopiev hammering his fists on the other boy. The fourth boy, face bloodied by Ivan, hit Ivan across the kidneys with his truncheon. Prokopiev grabbed the arm with the truncheon and broke it at the elbow.

And then he grabbed Ivan and ran.

It was the first time he had ever entered the city's sewer system.

To call it a sewer system implied something medieval. It was so spotlessly clean, one could have eaten off the tunnel floors except for the fact that maintenance personnel walked there. The tunnels only served as access to the sewer pipes, interconnected throughout the entire area of the Underground City's primary level.

With Ivan, he had worked his way nearer to the school, escaped the tunnels, gotten inside the school without the headmaster seeing them and without a further encounter with Boris and his friends.

Ivan had blood in his urine for the next three days, but neither of them was visibly bruised. The collar of Ivan's uniform covered the discoloration on his neck from where the paving block had struck him and, during physical training, Ivan was able to evade suspicious looks or cover the area with a towel.

Boris and his three friends were not so lucky.

Of course, to have told the headmaster would have been worse than anything.

So, they remained silent.

During a training exercise, not long after Ivan's death, Boris attempted to cut the rapelling rope of one of his men, a very good-looking young corporal who had apparently resisted the advances of his unit leader. But Boris only partially severed the rope and the young Corporal did not die. Everyone among the Officer Corps—junior officers at least—knew about it. Someone apparently decided that Boris was more a liability than an asset to the Elite Corps and when his rapelling rope was cut, it was cut all the way through.

There had been an inquiry and the death was officially listed as accidental. Walking quickly through the sewer system now, memories were Vassily Prokopiev's only companions. What would Ivan have thought? Prokopiev carried film given him by Marshal Antonovitch which could be used by enemies of the State, but for the good of the Soviet people. Would Ivan have called this treason? He didn't think so. Would Ivan have done the same thing? He thought so.

The pack he wore was heavy, but he had carried heavier. The weapons left for him were of the best quality. A vintage CZ-75 pistol, one of those which Antonovitch himself had likely ordered preserved in the gummy petroleum-based preservative known as cosmolene. Since these guns were still carried as prized possessions by many of the Officer Corps, handed down from father to son, their 9mm X 19 cased ammunition was still manufactured in limited quantities. Why had Antonovitch given him such a pistol? Was it some sort of symbol? If it were, Prokopiev could not quite fathom its meaning. The knife was one of the handmade fighting knives usually carried by officers who had never fought and never would, but finely crafted in the American Bowie pattern. The assault rifle was standard issue. For both the rifle and pistol, he was provided extra magazines and what almost seemed like too much ammunition. Perhaps the Comrade Marshal had assumed that he—Prokopiev—would have to fight his way out of the Underground City. And such a scenario was certainly possible because the sewer system only went so far and then he would have to exit the system and attempt to leave by one of the lesser-used entrances.

There would be guards. He outranked them, but they would wonder why he was in battle uniform and wearing field equipment and all alone. He would attempt to bluff his way through, that he was on some special mission. If that worked, he would be out without blood being shed. If it did not work, they would ask for his papers. Comrade Marshal Antonovitch had provided no such papers, could not have without implicating himself. Then it would come to a fight.

As he walked on, listening to the sounds of his breathing, the clicking of his bootheels on the flooring beneath him, he wondered if he could shed Soviet blood.

He knew he might have to find out.

Chapter Thirty-Two

Akiro Kurinami opened his eyes.

"Welcome back to us, Lieutenant," Damien Rausch said, smiling. "You had us all very worried."

"What—what happened?"

"You were apparently followed by Russian personnel. When you attempted to gain entrance to Doctor Rourke's mountain retreat here, you were struck a blow to the head. Colonel Mann sent us here, anticipating that you might come here. He sent us so that we could help you. It was very fortunate for you indeed that we arrived when we did."

"Where—ahh—were they?"

"The Russians? One of them escaped, the other going over the edge of the roadway and falling to his death at the base of the mountain. Can you sit up? We need you to open the inner doors to Doctor Rourke's Retreat so that we can utilize his radio and send for help. Our helicopter was forced down in the blizzard and our radio was destroyed. The Russian who got away has most probably already called for assistance. There is little time to lose." Rausch leaned over Kurinami, gently putting his hands to Kurinami's upper arms. "Let me help you to sit up."

"Thank you. Elaine—how is she?"

"Doctor Halversen, at last report, was perfectly fine. You have nothing to worry about on that score, Herr Lieutenant. Can you stand?"

"I—I think so."

"Excellent. But remember, should you feel faint because of that blow to the head, just sit down again. We will help you. You can easily tell me the combination to the doors and we can open them."

"All right. But I think I can do it."

"Good, Herr Lieutenant. I was told to expect a man of singular courage; and, indeed, you are that," Rausch told him. He helped Kurinami gradually to his feet, two other of Rausch's eight men supporting the young Japanese naval aviator, still wobbly on his legs.

Kurinami started toward the doors, Rausch's men helping him. The Japanese moved very slowly. At last, he stopped before the doors, nodded and smiled to the two men and they stepped back a pace. He began to work the combination lock on the left. "Two combinations?" Rausch asked, genuinely curious. "Was this the customary thing in your time, Herr Lieutenant?"

"Doctor Rourke is a very cautious man—Mr. Rausch, was it?"

"Yes."

"Why isn't it Captain Rausch or something?"

Rausch smiled. "You are quite astute, Herr Lieutenant. I am a member of a top secret group of intelligence commandos recently formed by Colonel Mann. We carry no military rank," and he smiled again, "although some of us did. I was, in fact, a—" Rausch hesitated, almost giving his SS rank designation. "—a Major. But we all serve the Fatherland in our own way."

"Colonel Mann is a fine officer. You are privileged to serve under him," the Japanese said, apparently finished with the first combination lock, starting on the second.

"He is an officer whose actions will always be remembered," Rausch said, but not adding why.

"Is your gunship disabled?"

"No. It was forced down, as I said. At least I do not think it is permanently disabled."

"If we cannot raise your base on Doctor Rourke's radio, perhaps I can get the helicopter airborne again. I have considerable experience."

"As I understand that you do, Lieutenant," Rausch nodded. It seemed that the second combination dial had been turned enough. "Are we ready?"

"Almost. Is Colonel Mann sending in reinforcements?"

"Oh, yes. When the Soviets attack, they will get more than they planned for, assuredly. I would venture to say, if you are feeling up to it, you will be right there among the heaviest fighting at the controls of your own gunship again." Kurinami would be dead as soon as he got the doors open and passed inside. Once it was clear that there were no passive defense systems within the Herr Doctor's facility, the Japanese's usefulness would come to its sudden, inevitable end.

"There."

"Now, how do the doors open?"

Kurinami looked over his shoulder, reached to the massive handles and jerked them, then pulled the right-hand side door open. "I'll go through first and get the lights."

"Yes—a good idea. We will be just behind you, my friend. Just behind you."

The Japanese disappeared through the open doorway. Rausch reached to his belt for his pistol, nodded to his men. He stepped into the darkness beyond the doors.

There were no lights. "Lieutenant?"

"Move and you are dead!" Kurinami's voice came from the darkness, somewhere ahead.

"What is this? To repay our kindness?"

"If you are who you say you are, step back outside and pull the doors closed and lock them. You will not freeze outside." Rausch felt for a wall, somewhere where there might be a light switch. "I will radio for help, confirm your identity and admit you to wait until help arrives."

"But, Herr Lieutenant, we cannot do that I am afraid. I have specific orders to contact my base as soon as possible." Rausch's hand found a switch. As he hit the switch with the tips of his fingers, he shouted, "Kill him!" He flipped the switch and nothing happened, no lights. One of his own men fell against him. There was a gunshot, the sound of a ricochet, Rausch firing toward the flash of gunfire, one of his men screaming in pain. "Bastard!" Rausch threw himself down into the darkness, on what felt like stone, his left elbow impacting too hard, his left arm going numb with pain for an instant.

"Herr Rausch!"

"Stay outside. Cover the entrance so he cannot slip out."

Kurinami's voice came out of the darkness, uncomfortably near. "I have visited Doctor Rourke's Retreat on several occasions. I know the floorplan. You do not. I have shut off all the lights. You do not know where the circuit panel is. Your only chance is to leave here at once."

"No—" And Rausch rolled onto his back, then rolled again, groping in the almost total darkness with his left hand. The floor fell away. He panicked momentarily, edged forward, felt a step beneath it. "You are the one who has no options, Herr Lieutenant. My eight men—"

"Seven—I hit one, Rausch."

"Very good! Seven. They have the doorway covered. You cannot leave. If you turn on the lights to get to the radio, to use it, you will be shot. Perhaps, as we exchange shots, the radio will be destroyed. I already have what I want. I have captured you and gained access to Doctor Rourke's mountain retreat and whatever secrets it may possess."

"Who are you?"

Rausch smiled. There was no purpose any longer served by lying. "My name is Rausch. I am still a military officer, but of the SS. My men and I are loyal members of the Party—"

"Nazis?"

"Yes, Kurinami. Nazis. And you and your friends and eventually all our enemies will be crushed. Surrender and I promise you a quick and honorable death. You have my oath."

"The oath of a Nazi? You must be crazy."

Rausch was tiring of the little verbal battle.

Rausch was ready to move, inched forward, aimed his pistol into the darkness where Kurinami's voice seemed to originate. "Lieutenant?"

"Yes?"

Rausch fired, again and again and again, the sounds of glass shattering, bullets ricocheting. Then Rausch threw himself over the edge of the steps, wriggling down them on his belly, the base surprisingly near.

Kurinami did not fire back.

"Lieutenant?"

There was no answer.

"Kurinami?"

Still no answer, but Rausch moved just in case. The only rational thing now was to wait.

193

Chapter Thirty-Three

She felt embarrassed because his body was so close to hers. "Forgive me, Sarah," Wolfgang Mann hissed. "In these mountains, I was momentarily uncertain of the origin of the gunfire."

She nodded, still trying to catch her breath. He had pushed her against the rocks, sheltering her with his body, the three men with them falling into firing positions around them. "No—I'm all right, Wolf."

The pressure against her already eased.

They looked up the road. "I could almost swear those sounds came from the Retreat. Where else could they have come from?"

Wolfgang Mann's eyes narrowed behind his snow goggles. In German, he issued rapid-fire orders to his three men, then spoke into his radio. When he concluded, he translated. "I alerted my pilot to be ready for whatever might arise. I also instructed him to order back one of the J7-Vs from my squadron, again to be safe. I would like you to wait here." Two of his men moved along the trail ahead of them, keeping to either side of it, their assault rifles ready. The third man waited with them. She looked at the third man. "You have not only yourself but the child you carry to consider, Sarah."

She didn't need him reminding her of that. "What if whatever caused those shots requires knowledge of the Retreat to set things right? Even just how to get inside it?" And she reached into the pocket of her parka as she removed her right glove, then extracted the Trapper Scorpion .45 the Mulliner boy had given her five centuries ago. She worked the slide, chambering the top round out of the six-round magazine.

"As you wish, Sarah. But, you must stay beside me."

She raised the little handmade .45's safety, clutching the pistol tightly in her hand.

"All right."

She walked beside him, toward the Retreat . . .

Akiro Kurinami's right hand opened and closed on the butt of the Colt. His own weapon had been missing when he awakened, the first clue making him suspicious of his benefactors. But Doctor Rourke had begun to leave a chamber-loaded stainless steel Government Model Series 80 .45 automatic and two spare magazines in a niche just inside the door, Doctor Rourke telling him of this when he—Kurinami—and Elaine had sought refuge there. Doctor Rourke explained how he had removed the magazine springs from all three of the Colt magazines, then baked them in the kitchen oven to properly heat-treat them so they would retain their resiliency fully loaded over protracted periods of time. He had mentioned as an aside that, of course, he had welded the magazine floorplates because .45 ACP magazines were habitually only spot-welded and could come loose from the magazine body at the most tactically embarrassing moments, spilling floorplate, spring, follower, and cartridges and leaving the shooter with an empty gun.

urinami remembered all of that.

The two spare loaded magazines were in his pocket. The .45 was still in his fist. And Damien Rausch, this self-proclaimed Nazi, was still inside Doctor Rourke's Retreat. He would have to fix that.

Slowly, not even an inch at a time, he crawled toward the kitchen counter. Between the counter and the couch was the narrowest portion of walking space. The kitchen was up three steps from the great room floor, and Rausch would most certainly have come down the steps—Kurinami hoped. Keeping the steps as a guide, he would move ahead. When he came in line with the couch, that would be the killing ground, Kurinami determined.

He kept moving . . .

The light that could be activated from within the foyer was on. It was red, and as it washed over the blowing and drifting snow outside the open main entrance at her husband's retreat, it gave everything it touched the color of blood.

She crouched beside Wolfgang Mann, his three men now even with them, the two point men alerting the Colonel that the Retreat's entrance was open, that there were an undisclosed number of men inside just beyond the open door.

"What do you suggest, Sarah?"

She licked her lips beneath the toque she wore to protect her face from the wind, her tongue inadvertently touching the fabric. "If you could have one of your men get up on either side of the door to cover us, then you and I and your third man—the Corporal here—could come up on the blind side—from the right?" And she gestured toward near the large boulder, rolled away now. "The boulder would give us

197

cover until just at the very end. We could get to the doorway before they saw us. Either that, or it'll turn into a standoff and it could go on indefinitely."

"You could also get shot."

"I'm aware of that."

"All right, then." He nodded and he hissed whispered commands to his men, two of them, the point men from before, splitting to right and left, disappearing almost instantly. But, of course, Colonel Mann's personal men would have been among the best of his commandos. And she had seen Otto Hammerschmidt at work often enough. Otto— Her thoughts filled with the fear that she had for Annie and Natalia and Otto Hammerschmidt. Were they alive still? She felt tears welling up in her eyes, sniffed them back. "Are you all right, Sarah?"

"Uh-huh."

Suddenly, Colonel Mann's two point men reappeared, flanking the main entrance to the Retreat. Wordlessly, she cursed herself for never learning more about the Retreat's other entrances. She knew how to use them as exits, not how to enter from outside. Even though they weren't designed for that—"Sarah—we will move ahead now."

She looked at Wolfgang Mann, nodded silently to him, ran beside him. She told herself the exercise was good for her pregnancy, healthy for the baby. Pregnant women in tribal days would have their children beside the road, falling out, delivering, catching up. This was nothing compared to that. She stumbled, caught herself, Mann's hand suddenly at her elbow, ran on beside him. They reached the boulder which her husband would roll away to begin the entry process to the Retreat, his home away from home for them as he had called it. She shook her head, a flood of memories of awakening there, suddenly remembering why she lay in something like a coffin, why there was a smell of gas from within the bedding, why stalagtites hung from the ceiling, why a waterfall raged at the far end of the great room into a pool. And then seeing her son and her daughter, grown to maturity, almost the same age as she. And the feelings she'd had against John. She wondered if she still had those, or had she just given up? Was that why he had gotten her pregnant, to say, "Forgive me?" or was it simply an accident? But with John Rourke, everything was always planned ahead.

She crouched behind the boulder, Colonel Mann beside her on her right, the Corporal on her left. His men, who flanked the doorway, advanced, directly beside the opening now on either side.

Mann was up, running, saying nothing to her, the Corporal beside her still as she started to move. As Colonel Mann neared the door, his two men stepped through, crisscrossing, Colonel Mann's assault rifle opening fire. Sarah reached the doorway. A man in white snowsmock and holding an M-16 raised the rifle to shoot at her. She ducked left, stabbing the little .45 automatic toward him, bullets from some other source whizzing past her head. She shot him twice in the face and he fell back against the foyer wall, eyes open, dead.

Colonel Mann stepped in front of her—she almost shot him by accident—and sprayed his assault rifle into another man. "Nazis," Mann shouted . . .

Gunfire. Akiro Kurinami saw a blur of darker darkness and fired, the .45 belching long tongues of flame in the near total darkness, a red glow from the main entrance all the light there was. A pistol shot came toward him and he dodged left, realized too late he should have moved right, felt sudden heat, then cold in his left side. He fired again and again, heard what sounded like a groan of pain; but, he couldn't be certain, so much gunfire from the entrance. He edged behind the kitchen counter, pushed the magazine release button and ejected, the partially spent magazine falling to the floor beside him as he put the new magazine up the well.

Powerful lights shone from the doorway now. He stabbed the pistol toward one of them, started to fire.

"Akiro? Are you in here? What happened to the lights?"

It was the voice of Mrs. Rourke. "Here!" The pain in his left side seemed to grow worse and he rubbed his left hand across his face, then fell forward . . .

Two whiskey bottles were shattered, but John would be relieved to know they were the counterfeit ones made for him by the Germans rather than containing real Seagram's Seven. There was a bullet hole in the back of the couch. There was a bullet hole in the copy of the last issue of *Jane's Infantry Weapons,* but only near the outside edge. Some of the natural stone was bullet-pocked, but somehow she was sure John would be able to fix that. And, as for the couch, Annie was a marvelous seamstress and, if she couldn't repair it, John would just get the Germans to make a new one for him, of course identical to the old one. Heaven forbid anything should be different than he'd originally planned. And the German Corporal was already sweeping up the glass while one of the other two men (the other stood guard outside) was cleaning up the spilled whiskey. Her kitchen—it was John's kitchen, always had been—smelled like a distillery with the broken whiskey bottles. And the Retreat was freezing cold, but she hadn't asked for the doors to be closed until they were certain there were no more than the eight Nazis. She had turned the lights back on from the master panel. The doors would have to be closed soon, or else the light spilling from the open doorway into the night could attract Soviet helicopters if any of their pilots had the nerve to fly in such a storm.

Akiro Kurinami lay on the floor, a blanket over him and the afghan Annie had crocheted under his head along with one of the couch pillows. His eyelids fluttered. He opened his eyes.

"You'll be fine. But don't move. You've got a broken rib unless I miss my guess," she told him. She smoothed his hair back, smiled down at him.

"Did—did I get Rausch, Mrs. Rourke?"

"We got all eight of them. Now, rest, please."

"Nine—nine!"

Kurinami's eyes closed and his head fell back. She checked his pulse. He was passed out. His chest began to rise and fall evenly. She realized he hadn't passed out, just fallen asleep.

"Sarah—does he speak German?"

"I don't think so, Wolf," she added, looking up. "You mean what he said?"

"Then why is it he said our word for 'no'?"

She looked at Kurinami. "Nine men," she whispered.

Chapter Thirty-Four

The black Marine Spetznas uniform was a decent enough fit, although a little tight in the chest. John Rourke closed the belt at his waist, a Sty-20 in the holster. The belt was too loose, and he cinched it tighter than the buckle imprint in the synthetic leather indicated it was usually worn. Beneath the uniform tunic were his two Detonics Scoremaster .45s. From the floor of the German gunship—he stood on the ground in the snow beside the open fuselage—he took the six-inch-barreled Model 629, holding it in his right fist for a moment. It was a fine gun, but he missed the Python. In fairness, the caliber was superior for his purposes. He slipped the .44 Magnum between the belt and the tunic at the small of his back, holsterless, positioned for a cavalry-style reverse draw. The twin Detonics mini-guns in the double Alessi rig. He slipped the shoulder holster on, then quickly grabbed up the Soviet outerwear, a parkalike jacket with a poorly designed hood offering no facial protection and too long and tight for proper freedom of movement. The Soviet forces under the sea would learn the necessities of surface warfare, given half the chance, he reflected. He hoped they wouldn't get that chance.

Fifty men, all or most of them burned alive, and from the nature of the fire their deaths were not fast deaths. Perhaps had he gone immediately toward the source of the smoke— Rourke left the coat open, so he could get to his guns. The LS-X knife would have to stay behind, but the little Sting IA black chrome was inside the waistband of his borrowed uniform trousers.

"We're all ready," Paul Rubenstein said, coming up behind him. John Rourke nodded as he turned toward the younger man, his fingers running through the inside of the borrowed uniform cap again. Hopefully the Russian hadn't recently had head lice. Rourke pulled it on. "You look good. Can't close the coat and get to your guns, right? I got the same problem. I figure I can keep the Schmiesser slung so it stays in the small of my back. Not too fast to get to, but I can get away with it long enough."

John Rourke looked at the sky. The snow fell, if anything, more heavily. He looked at the black face of his Rolex. If he kept his left arm down, no one would spot that until it was too late. He nodded toward Paul Rubenstein and the two of them walked toward where Jason Darkwood, Sam Aldridge, and a Lance Corporal named Lannigan already waited. Somehow, Aldridge had talked Darkwood into letting him walk at the rear, with his hood up so none of the Marine Spetznas unit would see his decidedly American black skin.

No one had been able to wear the Soviet Sergeant's uniform without looking obviously an imposter, so it was decided to have five men go in instead of six. The Sergeant was simply too large a man. Rourke had decided to let Darkwood do all the talking, since Darkwood's Russian sounded more like the Russian spoken by the Marine Spetznas, Rourke's own Russian having a too decidedly twentieth century flair to it. The situation reminded him of a comparison between the French language as spoken in Canada and in France, the Canadian version decidedly different.

As they joined Darkwood, Aldridge, and Lannigan, Darkwood said, "I enjoyed that helicopter ride, but it scared me half to death. I'll take submarines any day, Doctor." And he looked at the others. "Gentlemen, shall we? I think we all look very convincing in these admittedly rather tacky uniforms. Show time. Our public awaits." And Darkwood started out of the clearing and into the snow-crusted jungle . . .

The column of prisoners, ankles eighteen inches or less apart (judging from the shortness of their strides), hands behind their back, ankles and wrists bound in some sort of plastic restraints, Rourke imagined, slogged downward from the highlands toward the coast, through snow that in places looked thigh-deep. Not a man among them wore a coat or hat. Either they were stripped of their clothing as a further means of keeping them under control, or because whoever was in charge of the Marine Spetznas unit herding them toward the Island Classer enjoyed it.

The Soviet personnel, on the other hand, though almost equally weary-looking, were dressed in the same outer gear Rourke and the other imposters wore, and looked perfectly warm.

John Rourke looked at Jason Darkwood. "Captain Darkwood?"

"Yes. It's about that time, isn't it?" Darkwood looked at each of them, then started out of the trees, Rourke, Paul Rubenstein beside him, right behind Darkwood, then lance Corporal Lannigan, then Captain Aldridge. "Hoods up, gentlemen—don't want Sam Aldridge looking any more conspicuous."

"I'll remember this if we ever find a colony of black Russians," Aldridge groused. Rourke considered the concept: Pushkin, the famous Russian poet, was, of course, black. Perhaps Aldridge was clairvoyant.

And Rourke's eyes settled on the head of the column. Snow swirled like desert dust devils, blew in sheets like wind-driven rain. There were approximately fifty of the Marine Spetznas. Captain Aldridge's Marine corps personnel, what few there were, were in positions of concealment just inside the treeline on both sides of the Marine Spetznas unit's line of march.

Some would have called five men marching into the midst of fifty heavily armed enemy personnel suicidal. Rourke called it necessary.

Rourke slowed his pace, making his steps look more difficult, more laborious, to aid in convincing the Soviet personnel that he and the others had just walked several miles to intercept them. As John Rourke glanced at him, Paul Rubenstein did the same, Lannigan bumping into Rourke, then slowing. Their rifles were slung across their backs, out of easy reach, this to quell any suspicions the Soviet personnel might have. Rourke's left hand kept his coat closed, his right hand swinging free, the drawstring at the waist of the parka pulled tight, the loose end wound into his left fist. When he needed a gun, it would be easier that way. No grenades could be used, because of the proximity of the prisoners. Once the prisoners realized what was happening, even confined as they were, they might be able to help. But it was more likely some of them would be killed trying.

Darkwood signaled a halt, John Rourke clenching the drawstring more tightly in his left fist. He could hear Darkwood clearly as Darkwood spoke. "Comrade Captain. Our Sergeant fell and broke his neck. To have reached him, Comrade Captain, would have meant possible death for ourselves. He was so big."

The Marine Spetznas Captain said nothing for a moment, eyed them, then said. "Your name, Corporal."

"My name. Yes." Darkwood turned and looked

toward Rourke and the others. "Can you imagine that. He wants my name."

John Rourke cleared his throat. "Ahh—excuse me, Corporal. May I give it to him?"

"Yes. Go ahead and give it to him," Darkwood nodded, stepping slightly aside.

The Marine Spetznas Captain started to reach for his Sty-20 dart gun. John Rourke's left hand snapped outward, pulling the drawstring tight and the coat back away with it as his right hand snaked toward the small of his back, grabbed the Pachmayr-gripped butt of the six-inch .44 Magnum. Rourke knifed it forward, when it came to eye level, his right first finger already moving the trigger, Rourke saying, "Well, here it is." The 629 bucked once in John Rourke's right fist, the Marine Spetznas Captain's head seeming to expand, then suddenly contract as blood and brain matter blew out the left rear side of it into the face of the junior officer beside him. A cheer rose up among the prisoners. Gunfire was everywhere, Aldridge and the other Marine opening up, Paul Rubenstein taking a step forward, punching one of the Marine Spetznas enlisted men in the face, ripping the AKM-96 from his hands, spraying it as John Rourke fired the 629 again, taking down a Soviet trooper as he started to fire into the prisoners.

Already, John Rourke's left hand was moving, grabbing for the butt of the Detonics Combat Master under his right armpit, ripping it from the leather, the hammer cocking under his thumb. A Marine Spetznas Lieutenant was raising his AKM-96 assault rifle as Rourke settled the 629's muzzle again and fired, the Lieutenant's left eye gone, head snapping round, body following it in a spiral down into the snow.

The little Detonics in his left fist, Rourke fired, then again, one of the Soviet troopers going down. Darkwood was moving across Rourke's field of view, his Mid-Wake issue caseless 9mm pistol firing point-blank into living targets. Darkwood grabbed up a fallen AKM-96.

Rourke wheeled left, heard Paul Rubenstein behind him, the lighter cracks of Paul's Browning High Powers—he'd brought both of them. He and Paul had fought like this before. They would stand back to back, covering each other, killing. He could feel Paul's back against his back as he fired the 629 again, a 180-grain .44 Magnum punching through the throat of a Marine Spetznas Corporal. Rourke fired the little Detonics .45, at almost point-blank range, putting two rounds into the chest of one of the Soviets.

Gunfire was everywhere now. A Marine Spetznas officer tried to run toward a fallen trooper, grabbing up his rifle. John Rourke shot him in the chest with the .44 Magnum.

Rourke emptied the little Detonics .45 into an enlisted man who was trying to use his radio. The man fell.

A Soviet senior non-com charged toward them, his AKM-96 spitting lead or whatever it was they used with their caseless ammunition. John Rourke fired, the 629 empty as the 180-grain jacketed hollow point caught the man in the midsection, jackknifing him, his rifle discharging into the ground as he fell.

The 629 went into Rourke's belt behind his back, his right hand reaching for the AKM-96 slung across his back, his left hand ramming the little Detonics, slide open, into his pistol belt, then twisting up under his left armpit, ripping the second Detonics mini-gun from the leather. Rourke stabbed the AKM-96 forward and fired, a three-round burst, then another and another, men going down, the gunfire so intense around him that his eardrums pulsed with it. "Paul! Let's move!"

They had done this before as well. He would advance and Paul would advance, killing everything they could within the growing gap between their backs.

A Marine Spetznas enlisted man rushed Rourke on

the left. Rourke put him down with a single bullet to the throat, severing the spinal column. A Marine Spetznas officer pulled the pin on a grenade. Rourke shot him and the grenade fell to the ground, Rourke wheeling right, a double Tae-Kwan-Doe kick to the man's right side as he fell, pushing the body down over the grenade. Rourke shouted, "Grenade!" and threw himself left, impacting one of the Soviet troopers with his body, shooting the man twice, then a third time in the chest as they fell. The ground vibrated for an instant and there was a muted roar, chunks of body parts flying, flesh and blood and bits of bone raining down in the snow, the snow in a circle inscribed around what remained of the body washed pink as Rourke pushed himself to his knees. He emptied the Detonics mini-gun into a senior non-com.

The AKM-96—Rourke fired it out into three advancing Marine Spetznas.

The thing was turning around. Soviet personnel were fleeing into the trees.

John Rourke saw one man with a radio set strapped to his back. If he contacted the Island Class submarine, it was all over.

"He's mine!" Rourke shouted, throwing down the empty AKM-96, stuffing the empty Detonics mini-gun into his left side pocket.

He tore open the front of his tunic, his fists closing over the butts of the Scoremasters.

Rourke tore them free, jacking back the hammers. He started running, jumping the body of a Marine Spetznas, shagging off one of the prisoners who reached out to clap him on the shoulder. "God bless you!" the man shouted.

"I need His blessing," Rourke called back, running.

The man with the radio disappeared into the snow-blanketed foliage. Rourke charged in after him, getting a dozen yards into the jungle and stopping dead, listening, the cocked and unlocked .45s in both raised fists.

He heard the voice to his right. "This is Proletariat One, come in, Commander! This is Proletariat One—"

"Meet the people."

As Rourke broke through the foliage, the Marine Spetznas turned around, one of the miserable Sty-20 dart guns in the snow beside him but an AKM-96 assault rifle in his right hand. Rourke's Scoremasters bucked in his hands, then again and again, the body sprawling into the snow.

John Rourke dropped to his knees—beside the radio. He picked up the microphone, setting the pistol from his left hand into the snow, cocked and locked. "This is Proletariat One," Rourke said, trying to as closely as possible approximate the deadman's voice. "Over."

There was the crackle of static. Then a voice. "One moment." More static. The same voice. "Proceed."

Rourke almost depressed his push-to-talk button.

Then, "This is Commander Stakhanov. What is it? Over."

"This is Proletariat One. Upon orders of my commander, I am to advise you all goes well and the column proceeds toward the beach. Proletariat One Out."

"Stakhanov Out."

John Thomas Rourke threw down the microphone. He picked up his gun.

Maybe this Stakhanov had bought it, maybe not. Soon they would find out.

Methodically, Rourke began to strip the man of his coat and uniform and cap and pistol belt and boots, even the little Sty-20 pistol.

When he was all through, Rourke left the dead man in his underwear there in the snow and took the radio.

Chapter Thirty-Five

They moved through the tunnel for more than an hour before the tunnel suddenly began to pitch downward, steeply. Michael Rourke stopped Bjorn Rolvaag, trying to make himself understood. "If this tunnel—" and he made gestures which he hoped would help, thought probably wouldn't. "If it drops like this—where will it end?"

Rolvaag smiled, patted his dog on the head when it stood on its hind legs beside him. Michael petted Hrothgar, too.

"Michael? Where is this tunnel going?" Maria Leuden asked.

"God knows—and maybe Bjorn and Hrothgar, too."

They continued on, some of the German commandos and ordinary soldiers reiterating Maria Leuden's question, but no one mentioning that they should turn back.

They stopped, at Rolvaag's insistence, ate, Maria resting her head against Michael's shoulder. When the rest period seemed ready to end, Maria and the men, respectively, found isolated corners of the tunnel to answer their physical needs, then prepared to go on.

But Rolvaag signaled with his hands that they should not.

Michael just looked at him in the light of their flashlights, Rolvaag's eyes shining. Perhaps the head injury had done more serious damage than anyone suspected.

"Hrothgar!" And he pointed at the dog and the dog sat, its huge tongue hanging out as if it, too, were somehow mad. Then Rolvaag looked at Michael. "Michael!"

Michael Rourke wondered if somehow he were supposed to sit, too. But Rolvaag gestured him ahead, Michael calling back to Maria, "Wait here."

"Please, Michael?"

"Then stay beside me."

Maria Leuden fell in beside him, Rolvaag several paces ahead.

They walked on that way for what Michael estimated as a hundred yards, then suddenly the tunnel narrowed. Rolvaag turned toward them and raised the first finger of his right hand to his lips in the universal gesture for silence. Michael nodded.

Rolvaag moved into the narrow portion of the tunnel, Michael after him. No longer was it possible to keep Maria beside him. She moved behind him instead.

The tunnel seemed to be becoming progressively narrower and the ceiling lower, Michael bending his head slightly before it was really necessary, just the feeling of the tunnel somehow making it smaller, lower.

Again, Rolvaag stopped. "Light," Rolvaag said, shutting off his flashlight.

Michael Rourke weighed the flashlight in his hand. "Michael—do not."

"We've got to play this out," Michael told her, his voice a low whisper. "Just hold on to my belt and don't let go."

212

"All right."

He leaned toward her, kissed Maria's forehead. Then he shut off the light.

He could no longer see Rolvaag, felt Rolvaag tug at his sleeve, moved slowly behind him, the pressure of Maria's hand at his belt. His coat was open and he was still warm here. The tunnel made him feel as if he were smothering and he was not normally claustrophobic.

They seemed to go around a curve in the tunnel and everything was wider because there was no longer the pressure of the tunnel walls near his shoulders, brushing against his elbows. Michael Rourke squinted suddenly. As he fully opened his eyes, there was light, the purple lights of the grow lamps of the Hekla community streetlights. Coming toward him through a crack that looked no more than a few inches apart.

Rolvaag tugged at him to continue. Maria's hands touched at his neck, then her hand returned to his belt. He started walking again, almost able to see Rolvaag, almost able to see where he was going.

The crack of light seemed to grow slightly wider and he realized this was only because he was getting closer. The tunnel curved again, and as Michael came around the curve, he squinted again against the light. The crack was an opening wide enough for a man to pass through sideways.

Rolvaag quickened his pace and so did Michael, Maria behind him, then abreast of him, taking his left hand. In his right hand, Michael held one of his Beretta pistols.

Rolvaag dropped to one knee beside the crack, Michael flanking him, Maria beside him.

Through the crack, in the purple light, Michael Rourke could see the great park with its greenways and garden paths.

And Soviet helicopter gunships and armed guards.

213

Through this tunnel, through this crack in the volcanic cone, Michael Rourke realized he could bring a small army. He had no army. He had his commando unit and the volunteers. But outside, in the storm, there were more than two hundred and forty German soldiers and technicians. He could get at least half that many and not leave what remained of the German base totally defenseless.

"Hekla," Bjorn Rolvaag smiled.

He wanted to tell Rolvaag his thoughts, wanted to tell him that no, they would not penetrate through the niche of rock now, not when they could bring a hundred more fighting men.

Rolvaag looked at him, said, "Madame Jokli—my sister—friends. Wait me."

Michael looked at him.

Rolvaag took a cylindrical piece of metal from his mouth, touched it to his lips, blew into it.

"What is that, Bjorn?" Michael Rourke asked him.

"It's a whistle, Michael," Maria whispered.

There was a soft padding sound. It grew louder.

Hrothgar bounded out of the darkness. And Bjorn Rolvaag was up, passing through the niche of rock. Michael Rourke reached after him. But the only way to stop Rolvaag would have been shooting or stabbing him.

Michael Rourke looked at Maria. "Get the others. Bring them here. Wait for me."

"Michael—no!"

He kissed her hard on the mouth as he shrugged out of his jacket, grabbed up his M-16 and pushed through the niche, her hands reaching after him.

He thought he heard her call his name.

Beneath him, along a trail dotted on both sides with beautiful flowers and perennial shrubs, he could just make out Bjorn Rolvaag, swinging his mighty staff, his

214

dog bouncing at his heels. Michael Rourke followed him.

Michael could hear his father's voice inside him, warning him not to do something like this. But, at the same time, he could see his father, John Rourke, doing exactly the same thing, because there wasn't really any choice and he couldn't let Rolvaag who never even carried a gun do the thing on his own and die.

Michael Rourke quickened his pace so he could catch up. There were things to do . . .

Vassily Prokopiev reached the end of the sewer tunnel, took off his pack, sat there on the tunnel floor for several minutes, and rested while he collected his thoughts.

Above him lay the sewage treatment facility, where the exiting sewer water was treated and funneled into special piping systems for industrial cooling purposes. At any moment a sewer worker might come down into the tunnel system. Prokopiev would not have to kill such a person because the man or woman would be unarmed. Simply render him temporarily unconscious.

Above him, in the treatment plant, there were no armed guards, either. But a short distance outside the plant gate lay the westernmost exit from the Underground City. It was the smallest entrance/exit, used only for industrial purposes. The trucks which were now able to move freely in and out in the decades since the return to the surface carried out certain industrial wastes to the new chemical factory complex where, it was rumored, new types of gas were being perfected, tested. Beyond the gates, of course, there were military personnel everywhere. But he could blend in there. And there were places where gunships were frequently landed. He could steal one of these.

He physically recoiled at the idea of stealing.

But there was no hope of reaching the German lines without one.

He exhaled, stood up, pulled on his pack. He checked his weapons, a plan of sorts hatching in the back of his mind. If it worked, he might avoid the shedding of innocent blood. If it did not, he might die. It was not as if he were not already committed to what he must do. He was.

But the doing of it would be the most difficult task he had ever performed in his life. It was necessary to constantly reassure himself that this was right.

As he began to climb the ladder, one of the wounds he had sustained at the Second Chinese City suddenly pained him and he swung back from the ladder on his good arm. After a few seconds, the pain began to subside.

He continued the climb upward.

And he thought again about the pistol which the Comrade Marshal had given him, the sort of pistol a senior officer passed on to a son or nephew who would carry on for him.

What went on in the mind of Comrade Marshal Nicolai Antonovitch? Why had he—Vassily Prokopiev—been chosen? And what had the Comrade Marshal meant? He remembered the Comrade Marshal's words. "Tell Doctor Rourke this changes nothing. I would kill him if I had the chance. And I will expect the same courtesy from him."

Prokopiev kept climbing.

Chapter Thirty-Six

The water was as warm as the Pacific was supposed to feel, he supposed, or, almost at least; but the air temperature was in such sharp contrast that it made John Rourke shiver as he put head above water, oriented himself on the Soviet Island Class submarine as he sucked air, then tucked beneath the surface again.

Jason Darkwood had offered diving equipment, but as eager as Rourke was to try the wings and pressure suit and hemo sponge breathing apparatus, now was not the time.

And there would have been so few diving suits compared to so many men who would have to do without them.

Like the rest, he took his chances without one, surfacing as needed, gulping air, diving beneath the surface again, hoping not to be seen and shot by someone aboard the deck of the Island Classer.

He swam ahead, his knives his only weapons except for two of the Sty-20 pistols. As long as he lived, he would never get used to shooting people with a sleeping agent and having to wait for them to pass out. If a situation so deteriorated that one man had to shoot another, it was bad enough that the one who got shot should fall down quickly and the thing should end.

He kept swimming, Paul Rubenstein beside and a little behind him.

Rourke broke the surface again, gulping air, almost gulping water as a small wave lapped over him, tucked down again, Paul doing the same a second or so earlier.

The hull of the Island Classer loomed ahead like something out of a nightmare. When he had first seen one, when he and Natalia had been kidnapped and brought below the surface, he had thought it was that, something from a nightmare. But the nightmare was only beginning.

Rourke kept swimming.

He looked at the Rolex, having set the locking bezel in synchronization with Darkwood's watch, all other watches among the diving team and the surface team synchronized against Darkwood's watch, Darkwood's prerogative as ranking man. And John Rourke's Rolex read precisely two minutes before eight. He broke the surface again, the sky still gray when it should have been a rich blue here, early evenings in the Pacific beautiful experiences he remembered well. No longer. He tucked beneath the surface, Paul Rubenstein already down again, the younger man swimming beside him, pointing to his watch. Rourke nodded.

One minute. Darkwood and two dozen of the released prisoners, some of the men armed only with sharp sticks, surrounded Rourke and Rubenstein. At precisely eight in the evening, the remaining fifty or so freed prisoners, some of them wearing the uniforms of their former captors, and the Marine contingent from the *Reagan,* under the command of Sam Aldridge, now disguised as a prisoner, would begin to board the Island Class Soviet submarine *Arkhangelsk,* which meant that the hull defense and warning systems would be shut off.

If the submarine were to be taken, there would have to be minimal shooting. A submarine damaged beyond repair would be as useless to them as no submarine at all.

Jason Darkwood tapped John Rourke on the shoulder. It was precisely eight as Rourke glanced at the luminous face of his watch. Almost as one man, they broke surface beside the hull of the Island Classer, Rourke and the men surrounding him sucking in air. Paul Rubenstein seemed to be stifling a cough. In Paul's right hand was his Gerber MkI fighting knife.

Rourke's right fist held the Crain Life Support System X survival knife.

His eyes tracked Jason Darkwood as Darkwood moved along the hull, Rourke and Rubenstein beside him, following. Darkwood stopped, some sort of cleat in the hull. Darkwood looked to his men right and left, gave a thumbs-up sign, then began to climb, John Rourke swinging onto the cleats right behind him, Paul Rubenstein after him.

The cleats were not a ladder, but served well enough as purchases for hands and feet. There was a rail along the missile deck. Darkwood clung to it, roping along hand over hand, his feet only frictioning against the hull. Rourke followed him, his knife in his borrowed webbed belt.

John Rourke raised his head, peered across the missile deck. Some of Aldridge's people were already boarding the Island Classer. It was imperative to wait until some of them at least were below decks, lest the hatches were shut and the submarine dived.

Rourke kept moving, nearer to the sail, looking to his left. Half of the two dozen men of the boarding party were clinging to the rail, some of the others still on the cleats, fewer than a half dozen still in the water, men with knives bitten hard in their teeth, sharp

219

pointed sticks thrust through their belts, barefoot, shirtless men, like Rourke was himself, their bodies dripping wet, the wind like icy tentacles curling around them.

John Rourke kept moving. He stopped. It appeared that some of the Aldridge party were below decks. But there was some sort of altercation on the missile deck near the boat ladder on the starboard side, and Sam Aldridge seemed to be in the middle of it. The Marine Captain just stood there, still acting like a cowed prisoner, Lance Corporal Lannigan, now in a Marine Spetznas Lieutenant's uniform, standing between Aldridge and a naval officer of considerable rank, perhaps Commander Stakhanov from the radio message.

Rourke looked to his right. His eyes and Dark-wood's eyes met. Rourke looked across the missile deck. Aldridge took a step away, Stakhanov drawing a pistol. It wasn't a Sty-20, looked like a real gun.

Jason Darkwood shouted, "Board her!"

John Rourke pushed himself up, over the rail, his wet trousers sticking to his legs, his hair dripping water across his face, the wind and falling snow freezing him as on bare feet he raced across the missile deck. Lannigan stabbed one of the Mid-Wake issue pistols toward the naval officer and fired, again and again, the man's body tumbling back, sprawling across the deck.

John Rourke's left hand reached out, grabbed one of the Arkhangelsk's company from behind, spun him around. John Rourke's right hand thrust forward, the LS-X knife punching into flesh.

There were shouts. There was a pistol shot, then another and another. A burst of assault rifle fire and a scream, the body of a Soviet seaman tumbling from the sail, smashing down on to the missile deck. Rourke shoved the dead man off his knife, a junior Soviet naval

220

officer turning to face him, a Sty-20 in his right hand. Rourke's right hand moved faster, the LS-X slashing open the carotid artery, continuing across the throat, Rourke averting his eyes as the blood sprayed.

Paul Rubenstein was locked in combat with a man nearly twice his size, the man swinging a fire axe, Paul ducking under its arc, lunging with the Gerber knife, into the axe-wielding man's abdomen, out, then in again, falling to his knees as the man tumbled forward over him. Then Paul was on him, raking the knife across the man's throat as he snapped the head back by the ear, blood spurting across the deckplates.

John Rourke started for the sail, gunfire from the rail at its height, Rourke drawing one of the two Sty-20s from his belt, firing it again and again and again toward the man with the assault rifle, the useless pistol outclassed by the range. Rourke bashed it across the skull of a Soviet seaman, sheathing his knife, jumping for the ladder to the top of the sail. As Rourke climbed, the rifleman above him leaned over the railing, taking aim. He heard Paul's voice behind him. "John! Swing right!"

John Rourke swung right. There was the crack of a pistol shot from the deck below, then again and again. Rourke looked back, Paul Rubenstein, shirtless and dripping wet, the Soviet Commander's pistol in his right hand. Rourke swung back to the ladder, took the rungs as quickly as he could, vaulted over the rail, and was on the sail.

A yard from his feet, the main hatch was closing. To his left, a Soviet seaman rushed him with a monkey wrench. John Rourke sidestepped right, the Crain LS-X in his hand. As the monkey wrench swung, Rourke dodged, then rammed the Crain knife forward into the seaman's throat. Rourke brought his left fist to the knife, swinging the already dead man round, hurtling

221

the body off the knife and interposing flesh between the hatch and the deck.

On the deck near Rourke's bare feet was the AKM-96 that a moment ago had been aimed at him. He picked it up, stabbing the muzzle of the AKM-96 under their hatch. The body was being compressed, blood spurting from it. Rourke fired, spraying out the contents of the magazine into the space below.

He left the rifle wedged beneath the hatch, then reached to it, throwing his body weight against the hatch. Suddenly Paul was beside him, then Jason Darkwood. "Wait a minute!" Paul shouted. There was a second AKM-96 on the sail's deck and Paul grabbed it, fired it out beneath the hatch.

Suddenly, the downward pressure on the hatch eased, reversed. There was a shout from below. It was Sam Aldridge's voice. "We're secure below—get more men down here, Jase!"

As the hatch raised, Rourke, then Paul Rubenstein and Jason Darkwood simultaneously started down, Rourke's knife back in his fist.

Bodies of Soviet seamen and Americans from Mid-Wake lay everywhere. Aldridge was bleeding from his right shoulder. "The bridge is secure. And so are the torpedo rooms. Time's on our side now!" Aldridge started down into the bowels of the Island Classer.

Rourke took the ladder down, skating it, crashing, dropping to his knees, then running after Sam Aldridge.

Paul Rubenstein was beside him.

Sam Aldridge was shouting, "The ship is ours!"

And Jason Darkwood ran toward the bridge . . .

The fighting below decks consumed another hour, scouring every berth and cabin, every possible space for Soviet personnel. Those who surrendered or were captured alive were allowed to live. They were put ashore with provisions and a radio, the radio disassembled so it would take several hours to make it work again, enough time for Darkwood to pilot the Island Classer out of harm's way.

They waited for dawn, and the snow finally slowed, nearly stopped. There was a crack in the horizon, sun bleeding beneath it across the sea.

Above the sail, some of Aldridge's Marines raised the American flag.

John Rourke stood beside Paul Rubenstein. It was cold. The wind blew fiercely as the flag stiffened under it.

John Rourke watched it for a long time.

Things were turning around. He felt it inside himself. Beside him, Paul Rubenstein wept.